Walt Disney's Donald Duck in The Hada House

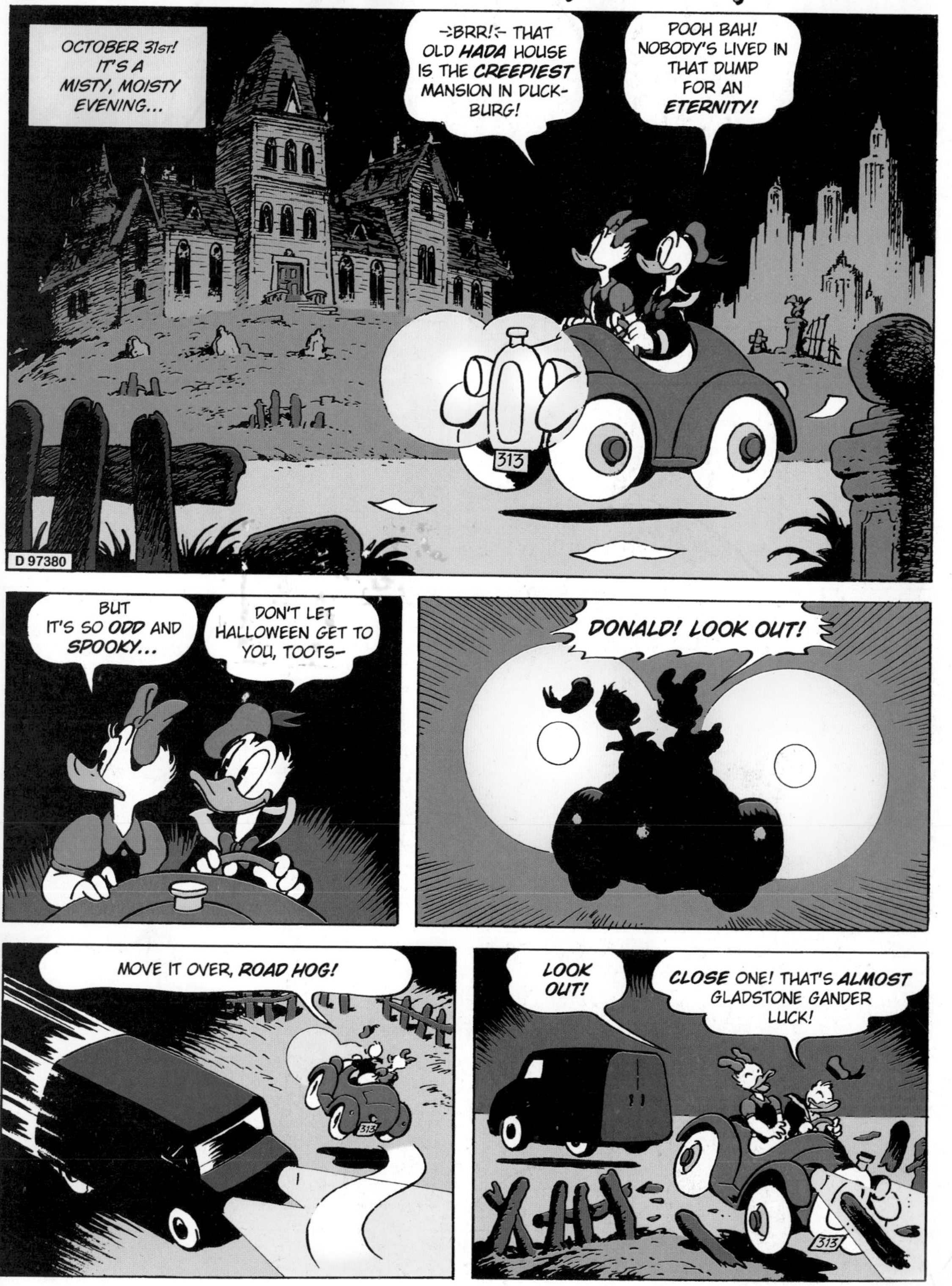
OCTOBER 31st! IT'S A MISTY, MOISTY EVENING...
–BRR!– THAT OLD HADA HOUSE IS THE CREEPIEST MANSION IN DUCK-BURG!
POOH BAH! NOBODY'S LIVED IN THAT DUMP FOR AN ETERNITY!
313
D 97380
BUT IT'S SO ODD AND SPOOKY...
DON'T LET HALLOWEEN GET TO YOU, TOOTS–
DONALD! LOOK OUT!
MOVE IT OVER, ROAD HOG!
313
LOOK OUT!
CLOSE ONE! THAT'S ALMOST GLADSTONE GANDER LUCK!
313

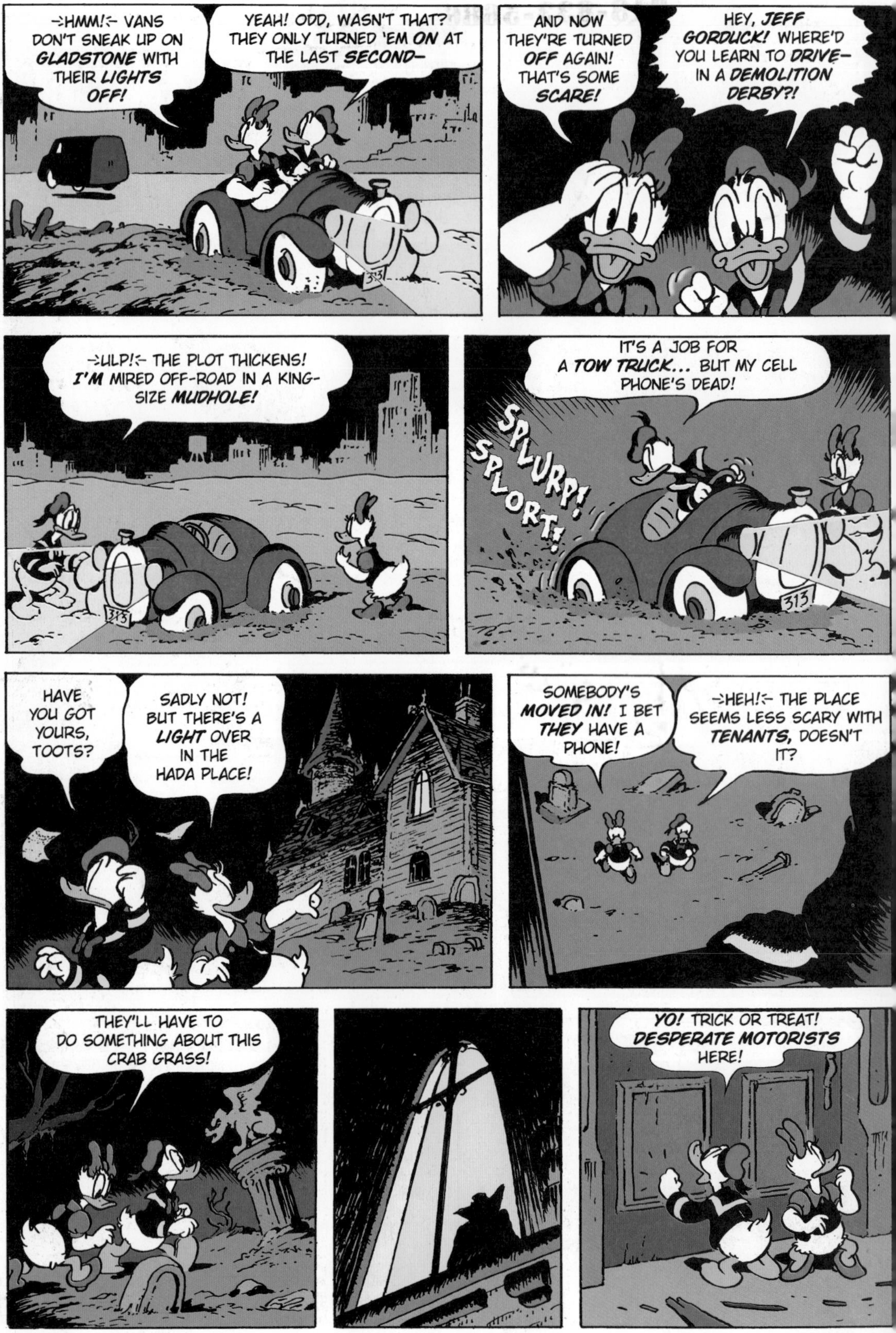

-HMM!- VANS DON'T SNEAK UP ON GLADSTONE WITH THEIR LIGHTS OFF!
YEAH! ODD, WASN'T THAT? THEY ONLY TURNED 'EM ON AT THE LAST SECOND—
AND NOW THEY'RE TURNED OFF AGAIN! THAT'S SOME SCARE!
HEY, JEFF GORDUCK! WHERE'D YOU LEARN TO DRIVE— IN A DEMOLITION DERBY?!
-ULP!- THE PLOT THICKENS! I'M MIRED OFF-ROAD IN A KING-SIZE MUDHOLE!
313
IT'S A JOB FOR A TOW TRUCK... BUT MY CELL PHONE'S DEAD!
SPLURP! SPLORT!
313
HAVE YOU GOT YOURS, TOOTS?
SADLY NOT! BUT THERE'S A LIGHT OVER IN THE HADA PLACE!
SOMEBODY'S MOVED IN! I BET THEY HAVE A PHONE!
-HEH!- THE PLACE SEEMS LESS SCARY WITH TENANTS, DOESN'T IT?
THEY'LL HAVE TO DO SOMETHING ABOUT THIS CRAB GRASS!
YO! TRICK OR TREAT! DESPERATE MOTORISTS HERE!

35674046794526

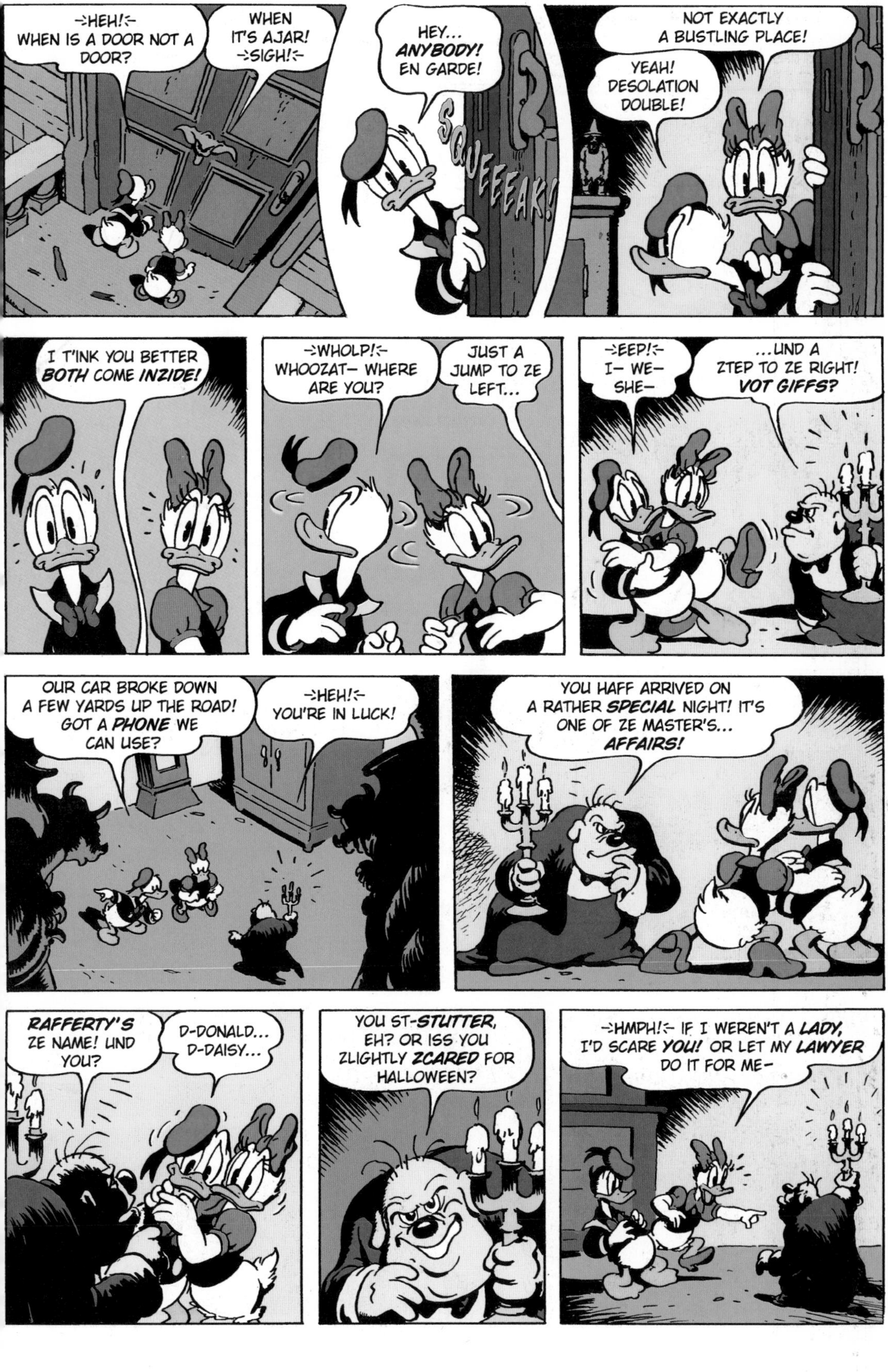

-HEH!- WHEN IS A DOOR NOT A DOOR?
WHEN IT'S AJAR! -SIGH!-
HEY... ANYBODY! EN GARDE!
SQUEEEEAK!
NOT EXACTLY A BUSTLING PLACE!
YEAH! DESOLATION DOUBLE!
I T'INK YOU BETTER BOTH COME INZIDE!
-WHOLP!- WHOOZAT- WHERE ARE YOU?
JUST A JUMP TO ZE LEFT...
-EEP!- I- WE- SHE-
...UND A ZTEP TO ZE RIGHT! VOT GIFFS?
OUR CAR BROKE DOWN A FEW YARDS UP THE ROAD! GOT A PHONE WE CAN USE?
-HEH!- YOU'RE IN LUCK!
YOU HAFF ARRIVED ON A RATHER SPECIAL NIGHT! IT'S ONE OF ZE MASTER'S... AFFAIRS!
RAFFERTY'S ZE NAME! UND YOU?
D-DONALD... D-DAISY...
YOU ST-STUTTER, EH? OR ISS YOU ZLIGHTLY ZCARED FOR HALLOWEEN?
-HMPH!- IF I WEREN'T A LADY, I'D SCARE YOU! OR LET MY LAWYER DO IT FOR ME-

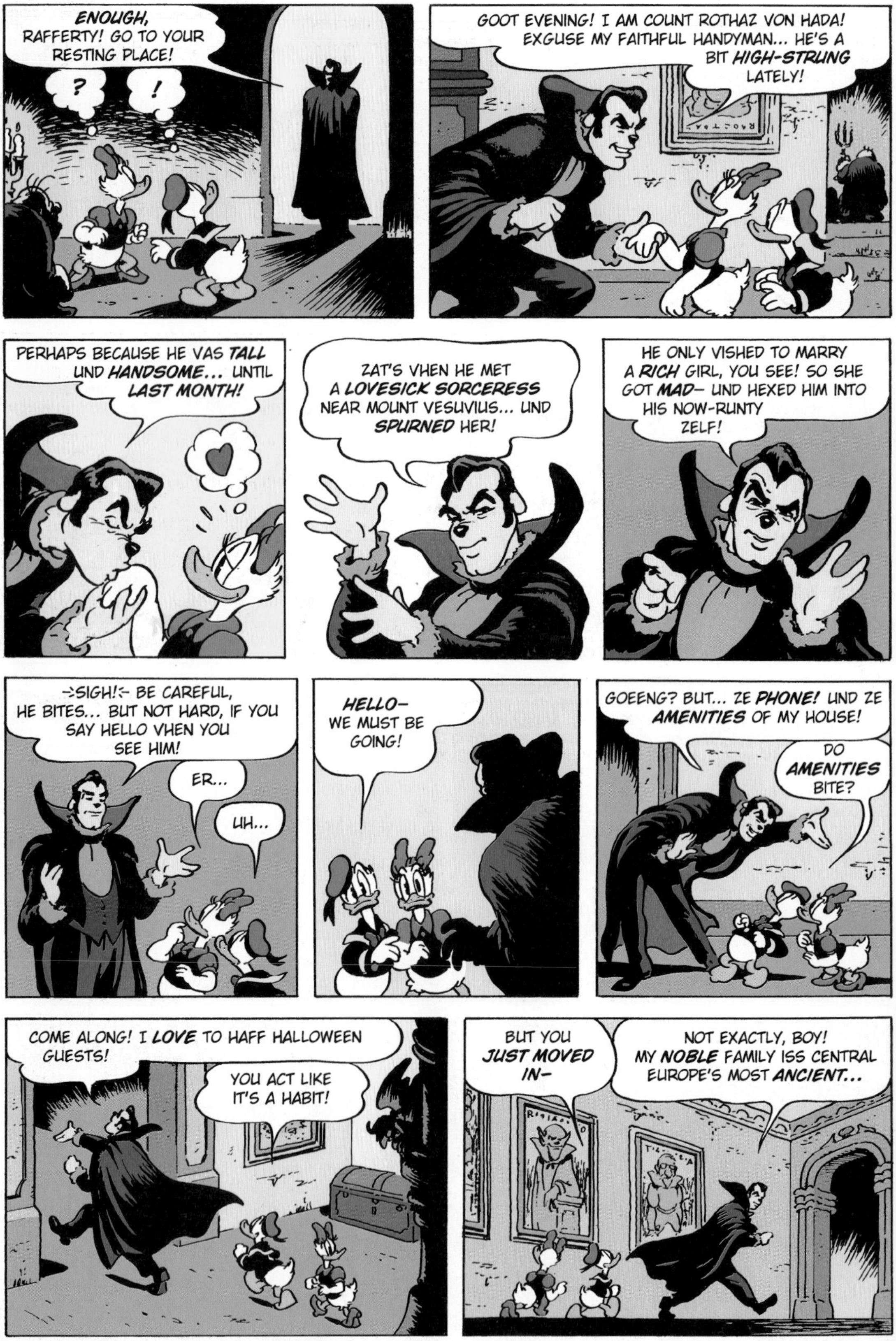
ENOUGH, RAFFERTY! GO TO YOUR RESTING PLACE!
?
!
GOOT EVENING! I AM COUNT ROTHAZ VON HADA! EXGUSE MY FAITHFUL HANDYMAN... HE'S A BIT HIGH-STRUNG LATELY!
PERHAPS BECAUSE HE VAS TALL UND HANDSOME... UNTIL LAST MONTH!
ZAT'S VHEN HE MET A LOVESICK SORCERESS NEAR MOUNT VESUVIUS... UND SPURNED HER!
HE ONLY VISHED TO MARRY A RICH GIRL, YOU SEE! SO SHE GOT MAD— UND HEXED HIM INTO HIS NOW-RUNTY ZELF!
-SIGH!- BE CAREFUL, HE BITES... BUT NOT HARD, IF YOU SAY HELLO VHEN YOU SEE HIM!
ER...
UH...
HELLO— WE MUST BE GOING!
GOEENG? BUT... ZE PHONE! UND ZE AMENITIES OF MY HOUSE!
DO AMENITIES BITE?
COME ALONG! I LOVE TO HAFF HALLOWEEN GUESTS!
YOU ACT LIKE IT'S A HABIT!
BUT YOU JUST MOVED IN—
NOT EXACTLY, BOY! MY NOBLE FAMILY ISS CENTRAL EUROPE'S MOST ANCIENT...

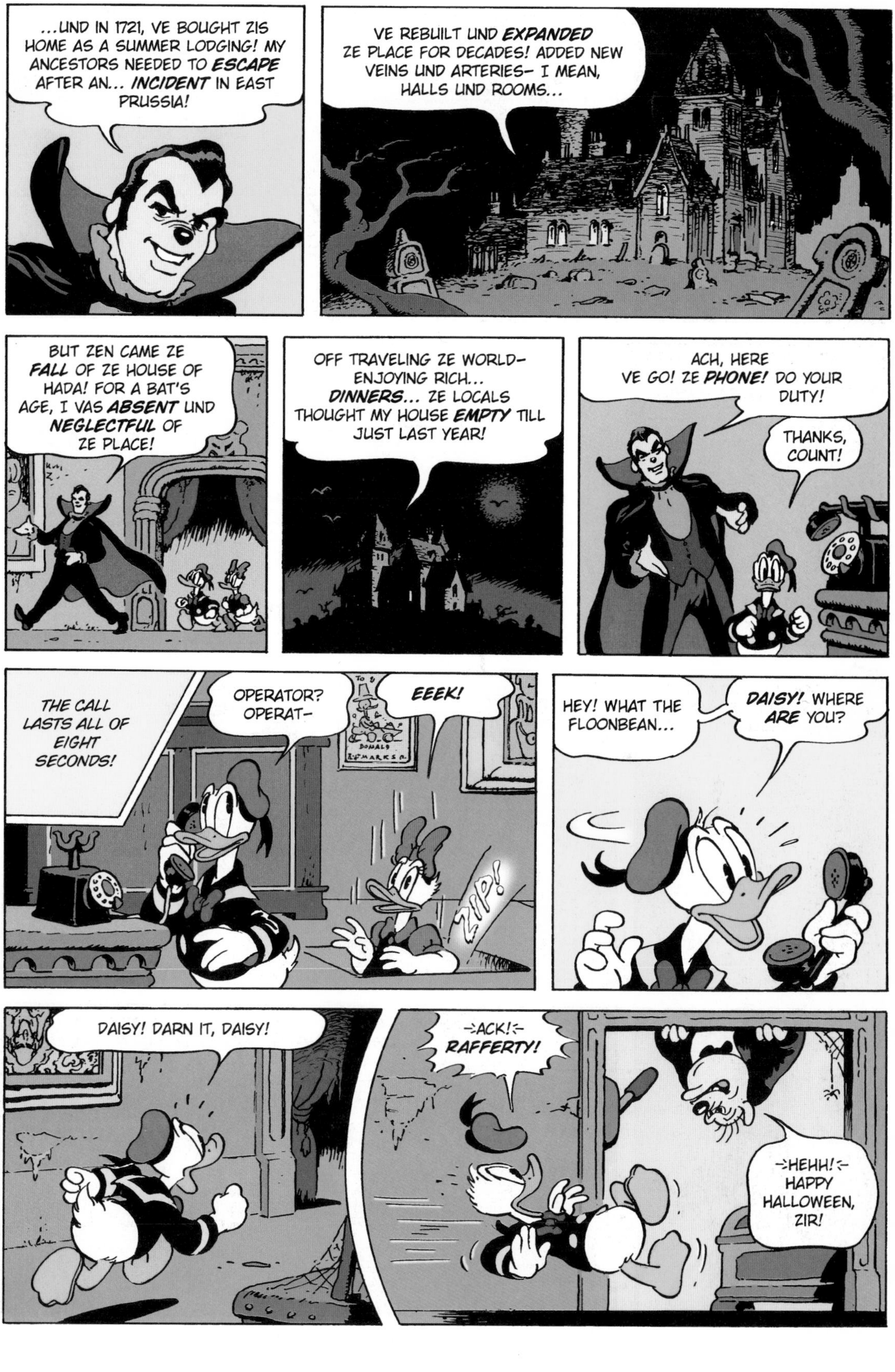
...UND IN 1721, VE BOUGHT ZIS HOME AS A SUMMER LODGING! MY ANCESTORS NEEDED TO ESCAPE AFTER AN... INCIDENT IN EAST PRUSSIA!
VE REBUILT UND EXPANDED ZE PLACE FOR DECADES! ADDED NEW VEINS UND ARTERIES– I MEAN, HALLS UND ROOMS...
BUT ZEN CAME ZE FALL OF ZE HOUSE OF HADA! FOR A BAT'S AGE, I VAS ABSENT UND NEGLECTFUL OF ZE PLACE!
OFF TRAVELING ZE WORLD– ENJOYING RICH... DINNERS... ZE LOCALS THOUGHT MY HOUSE EMPTY TILL JUST LAST YEAR!
ACH, HERE VE GO! ZE PHONE! DO YOUR DUTY!
THANKS, COUNT!
THE CALL LASTS ALL OF EIGHT SECONDS!
OPERATOR? OPERAT–
EEEK!
ZIP!
HEY! WHAT THE FLOONBEAN...
DAISY! WHERE ARE YOU?
DAISY! DARN IT, DAISY!
–ACK!– RAFFERTY!
–HEHH!– HAPPY HALLOWEEN, ZIR!

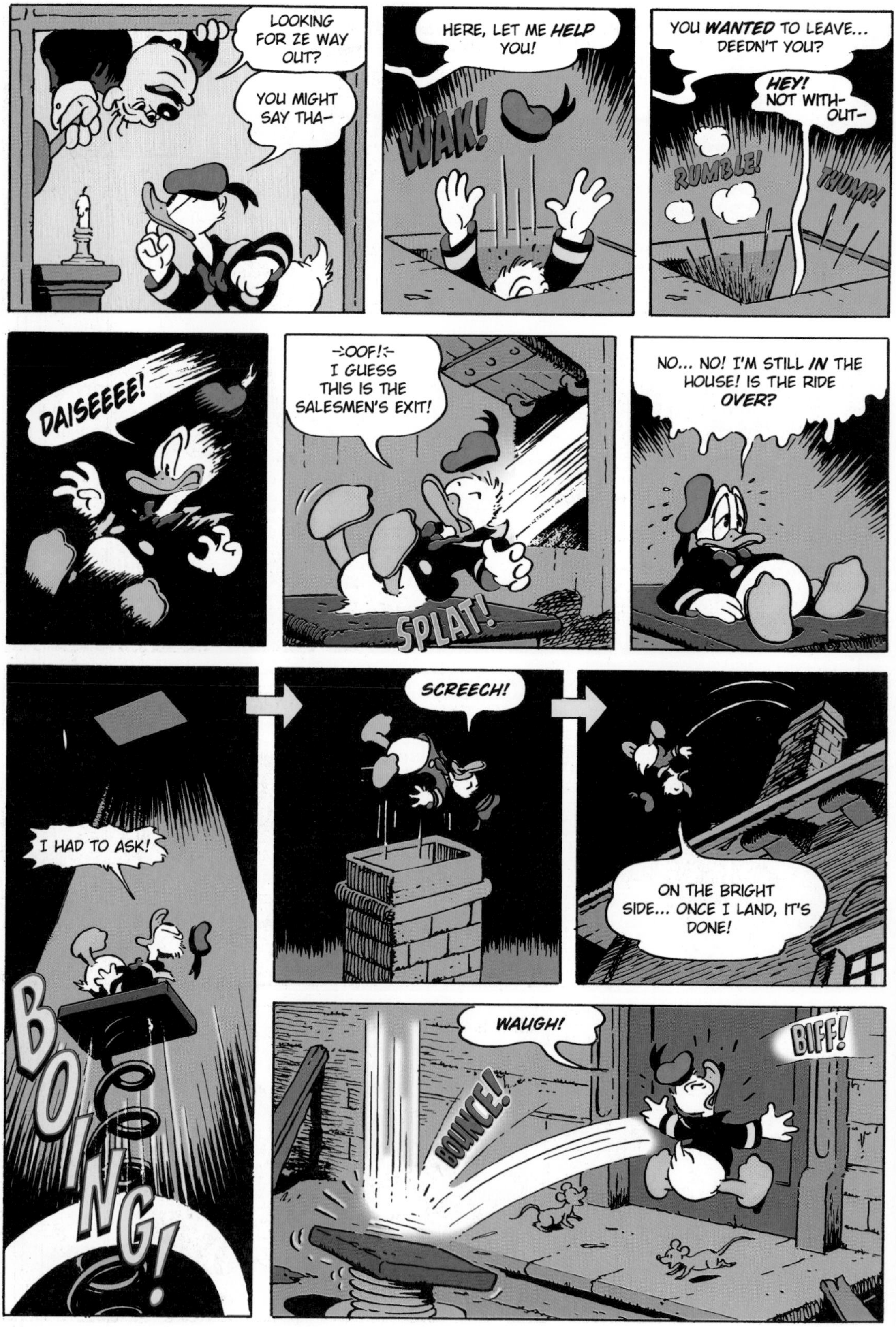
LOOKING FOR ZE WAY OUT?
YOU MIGHT SAY THA-
HERE, LET ME HELP YOU!
WAK!
YOU WANTED TO LEAVE... DEEDN'T YOU?
HEY! NOT WITH-OUT-
RUMBLE!
THUMP!
DAISEEEE!
-OOF!- I GUESS THIS IS THE SALESMEN'S EXIT!
SPLAT!
NO... NO! I'M STILL IN THE HOUSE! IS THE RIDE OVER?
I HAD TO ASK!
BOING!
SCREECH!
ON THE BRIGHT SIDE... ONCE I LAND, IT'S DONE!
WAUGH!
BIFF!
BOUNCE!

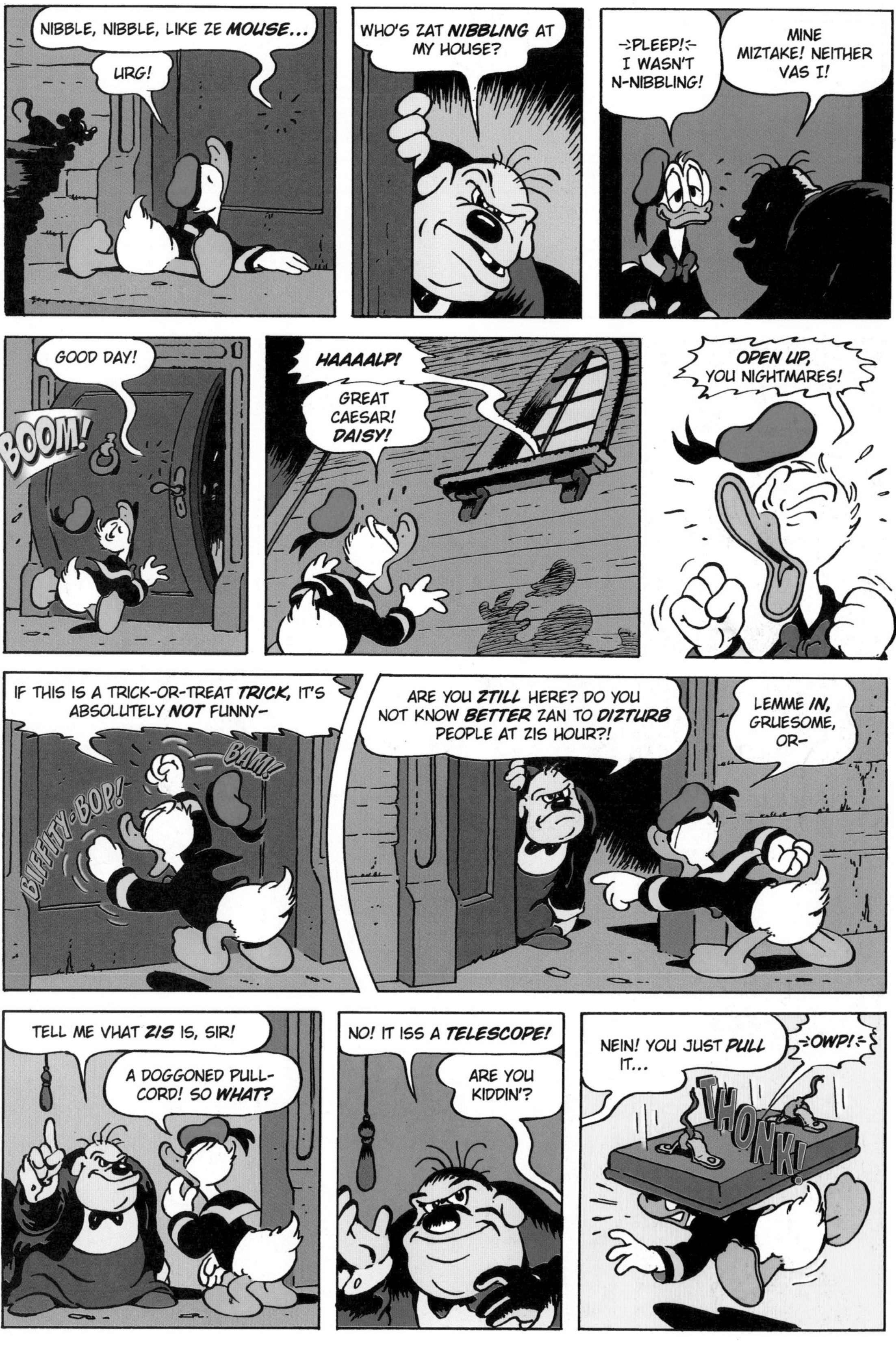

NIBBLE, NIBBLE, LIKE ZE MOUSE...
URG!
WHO'S ZAT NIBBLING AT MY HOUSE?
⇒PLEEP!⇐ I WASN'T N-NIBBLING!
MINE MIZTAKE! NEITHER VAS I!
GOOD DAY!
BOOM!
HAAAAALP!
GREAT CAESAR! DAISY!
OPEN UP, YOU NIGHTMARES!
IF THIS IS A TRICK-OR-TREAT TRICK, IT'S ABSOLUTELY NOT FUNNY—
BAM!
BIFFITY-BOP!
ARE YOU ZTILL HERE? DO YOU NOT KNOW BETTER ZAN TO DIZTURB PEOPLE AT ZIS HOUR?!
LEMME IN, GRUESOME, OR—
TELL ME VHAT ZIS IS, SIR!
A DOGGONED PULL-CORD! SO WHAT?
NO! IT ISS A TELESCOPE!
ARE YOU KIDDIN'?
NEIN! YOU JUST PULL IT...
⇒OWP!⇐
THONK!

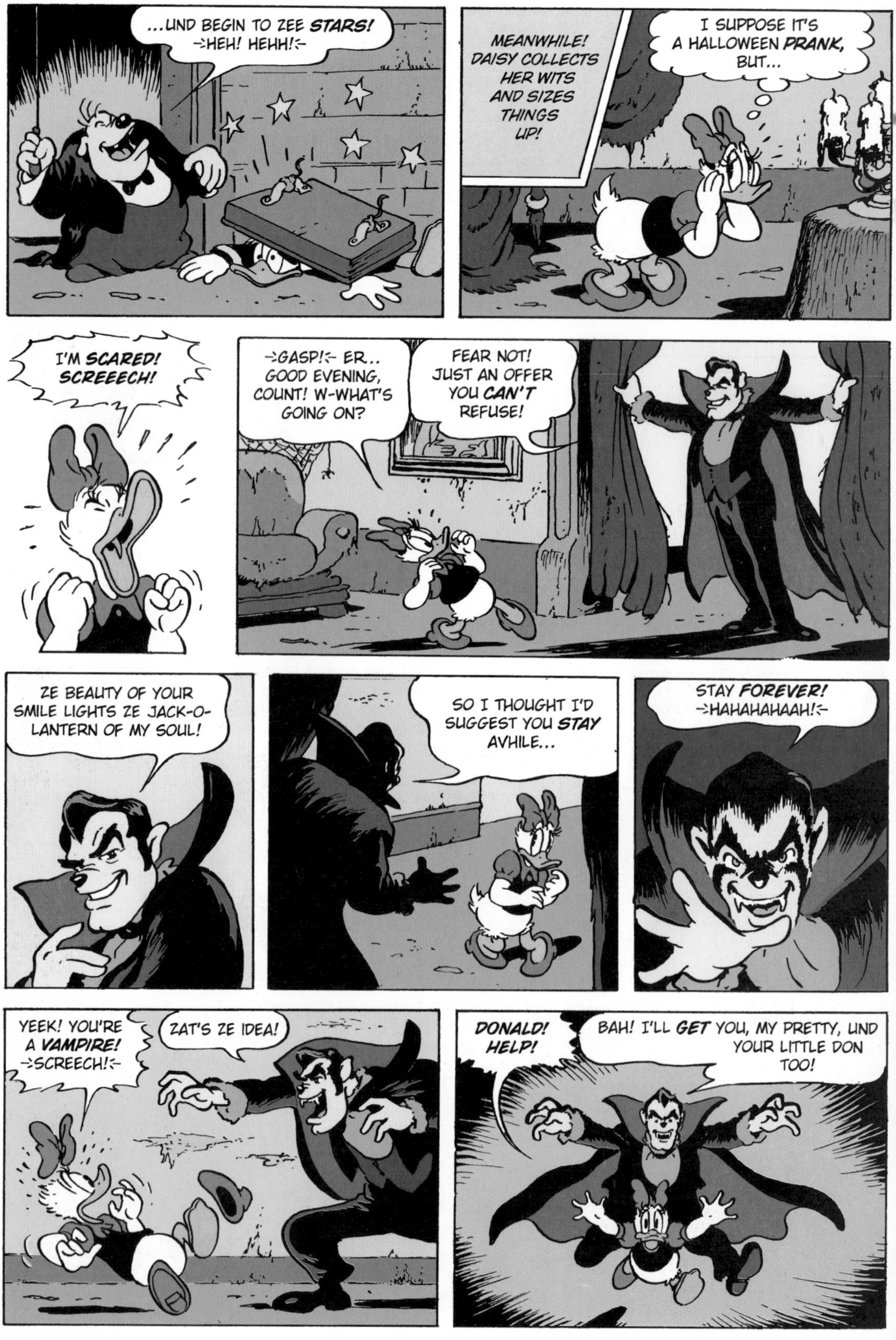
...UND BEGIN TO ZEE STARS! -HEH! HEHH!-
MEANWHILE! DAISY COLLECTS HER WITS AND SIZES THINGS UP!
I SUPPOSE IT'S A HALLOWEEN PRANK, BUT...
I'M SCARED! SCREEECH!
-GASP!- ER.. GOOD EVENING, COUNT! W-WHAT'S GOING ON?
FEAR NOT! JUST AN OFFER YOU CAN'T REFUSE!
ZE BEAUTY OF YOUR SMILE LIGHTS ZE JACK-O-LANTERN OF MY SOUL!
SO I THOUGHT I'D SUGGEST YOU STAY AVHILE...
STAY FOREVER! -HAHAHAHAAH!-
YEEK! YOU'RE A VAMPIRE! -SCREECH!-
ZAT'S ZE IDEA!
DONALD! HELP!
BAH! I'LL GET YOU, MY PRETTY, UND YOUR LITTLE DON TOO!

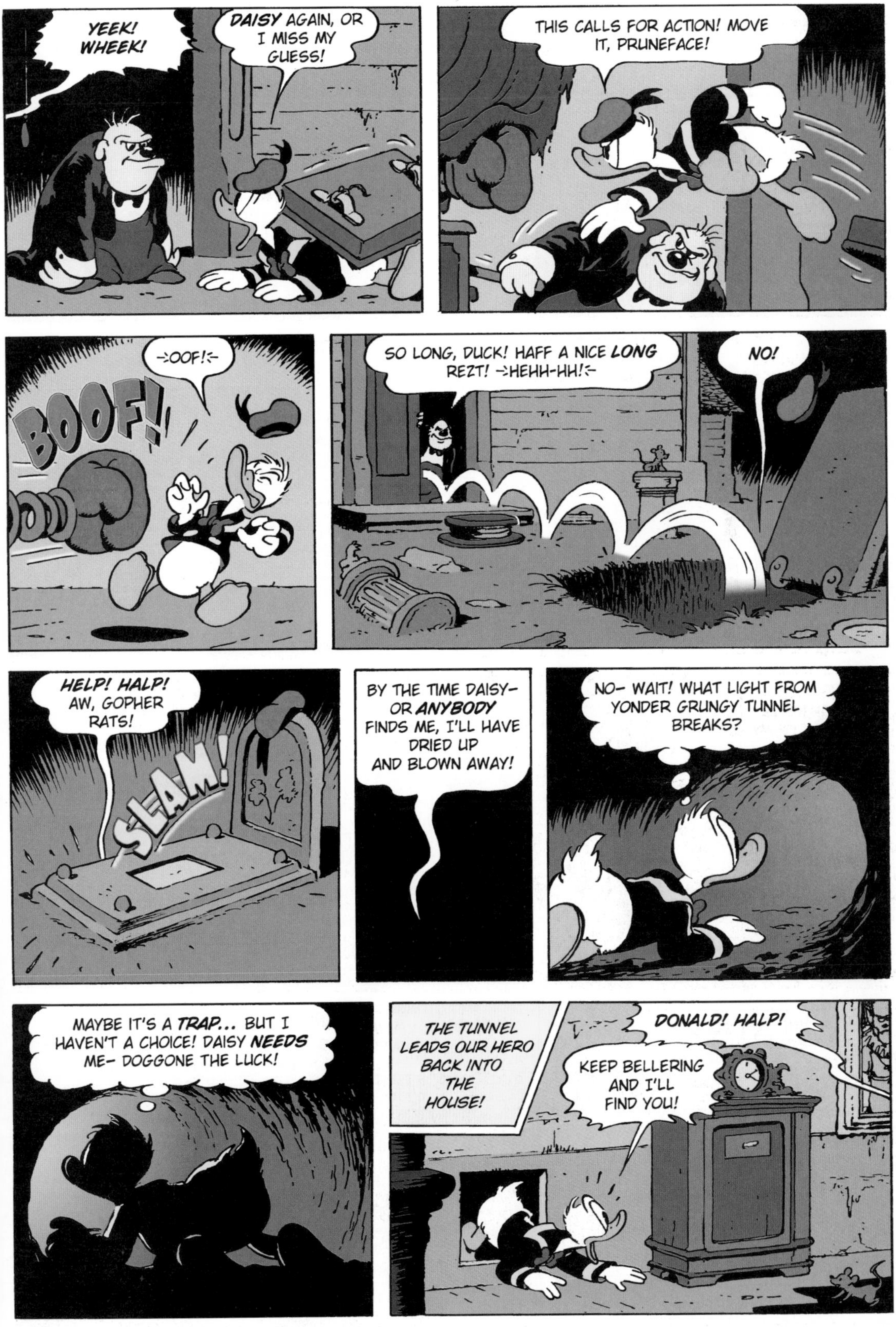
YEEK! WHEEK!
DAISY AGAIN, OR I MISS MY GUESS!
THIS CALLS FOR ACTION! MOVE IT, PRUNEFACE!
BOOF!
-OOF!-
SO LONG, DUCK! HAFF A NICE LONG REZT! -HEHH-HH!-
NO!
HELP! HALP! AW, GOPHER RATS!
SLAM!
BY THE TIME DAISY- OR ANYBODY FINDS ME, I'LL HAVE DRIED UP AND BLOWN AWAY!
NO- WAIT! WHAT LIGHT FROM YONDER GRUNGY TUNNEL BREAKS?
MAYBE IT'S A TRAP... BUT I HAVEN'T A CHOICE! DAISY NEEDS ME- DOGGONE THE LUCK!
THE TUNNEL LEADS OUR HERO BACK INTO THE HOUSE!
DONALD! HALP!
KEEP BELLERING AND I'LL FIND YOU!

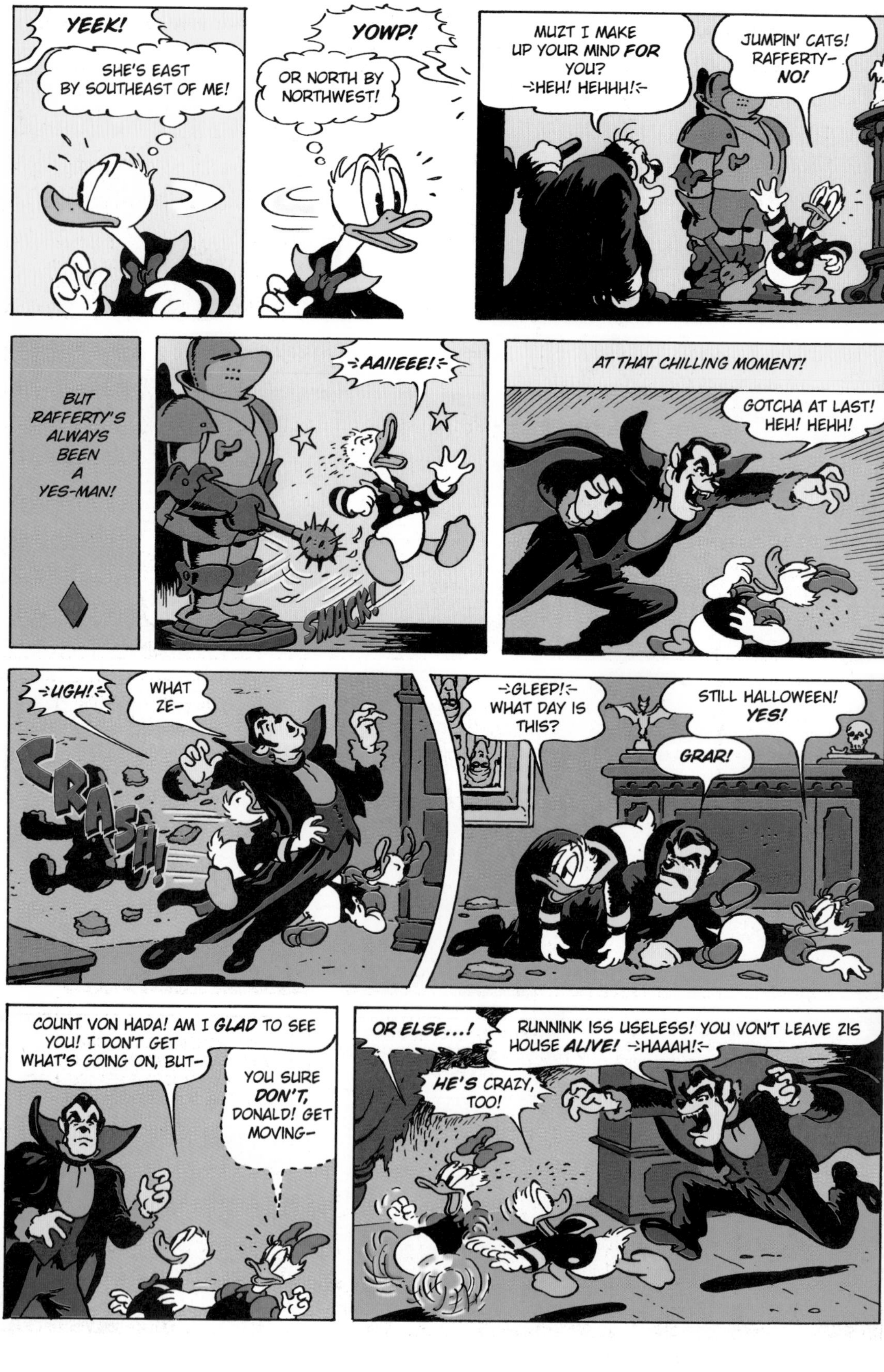
YEEK!
SHE'S EAST BY SOUTHEAST OF ME!
YOWP!
OR NORTH BY NORTHWEST!
MUZT I MAKE UP YOUR MIND FOR YOU? -HEH! HEHHH!-
JUMPIN' CATS! RAFFERTY- NO!
BUT RAFFERTY'S ALWAYS BEEN A YES-MAN!
-AAIIEEE!-
SMACK!
AT THAT CHILLING MOMENT!
GOTCHA AT LAST! HEH! HEHH!
-UGH!-
WHAT ZE-
CRASH!
-GLEEP!- WHAT DAY IS THIS?
STILL HALLOWEEN! YES!
GRAR!
COUNT VON HADA! AM I GLAD TO SEE YOU! I DON'T GET WHAT'S GOING ON, BUT-
YOU SURE DON'T, DONALD! GET MOVING-
OR ELSE...!
RUNNINK ISS USELESS! YOU VON'T LEAVE ZIS HOUSE ALIVE! -HAAAH!-
HE'S CRAZY, TOO!

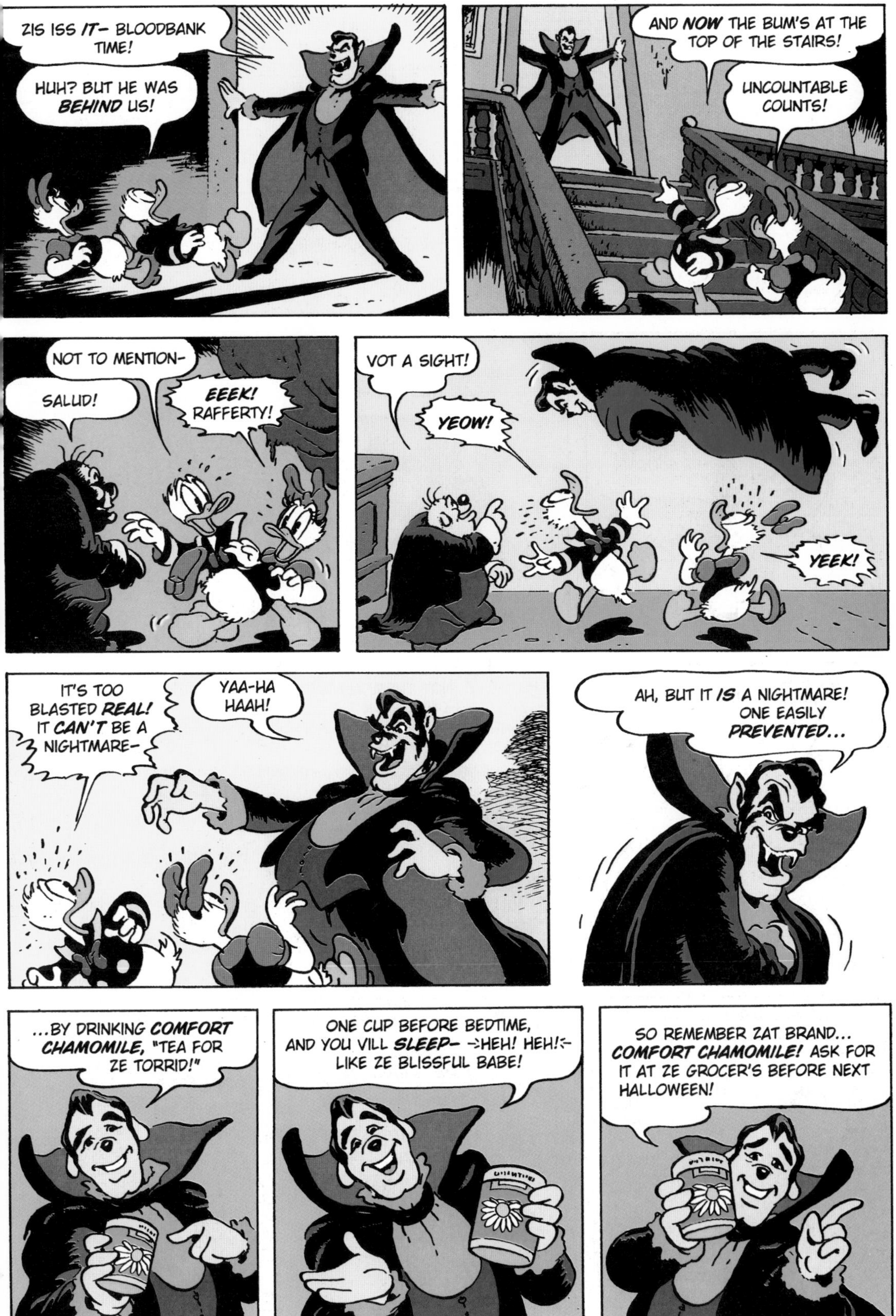

ZIS ISS IT– BLOODBANK TIME!
HUH? BUT HE WAS BEHIND US!
AND NOW THE BUM'S AT THE TOP OF THE STAIRS!
UNCOUNTABLE COUNTS!
NOT TO MENTION–
SALUD!
EEEK! RAFFERTY!
VOT A SIGHT!
YEOW!
YEEK!
IT'S TOO BLASTED REAL! IT CAN'T BE A NIGHTMARE–
YAA-HA HAAH!
AH, BUT IT IS A NIGHTMARE! ONE EASILY PREVENTED...
...BY DRINKING COMFORT CHAMOMILE, "TEA FOR ZE TORRID!"
ONE CUP BEFORE BEDTIME, AND YOU VILL SLEEP– HEH! HEH! LIKE ZE BLISSFUL BABE!
SO REMEMBER ZAT BRAND... COMFORT CHAMOMILE! ASK FOR IT AT ZE GROCER'S BEFORE NEXT HALLOWEEN!

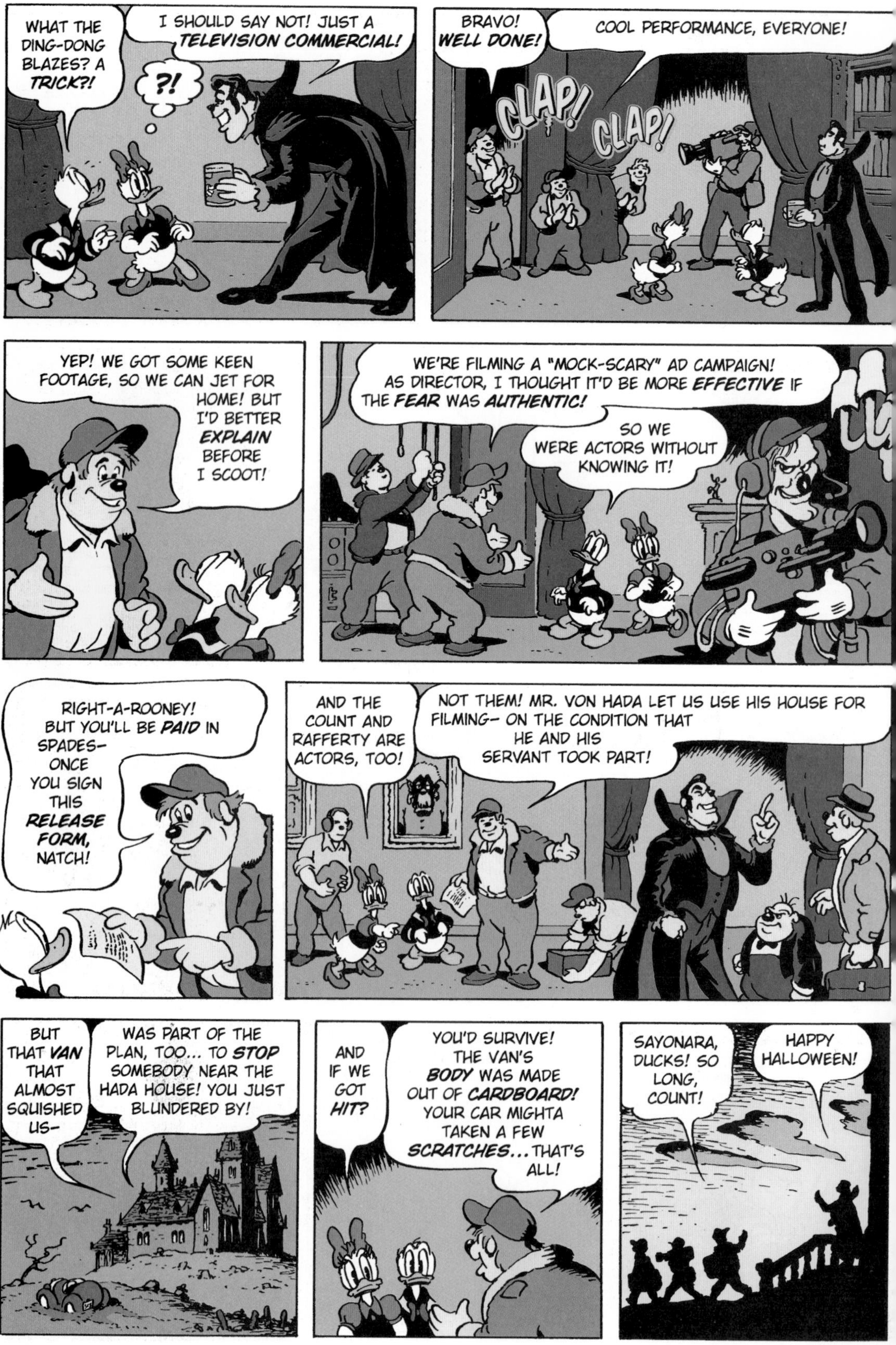
WHAT THE DING-DONG BLAZES? A TRICK?!
I SHOULD SAY NOT! JUST A TELEVISION COMMERCIAL!
?!
BRAVO! WELL DONE!
COOL PERFORMANCE, EVERYONE!
CLAP! CLAP!
YEP! WE GOT SOME KEEN FOOTAGE, SO WE CAN JET FOR HOME! BUT I'D BETTER EXPLAIN BEFORE I SCOOT!
WE'RE FILMING A "MOCK-SCARY" AD CAMPAIGN! AS DIRECTOR, I THOUGHT IT'D BE MORE EFFECTIVE IF THE FEAR WAS AUTHENTIC!
SO WE WERE ACTORS WITHOUT KNOWING IT!
RIGHT-A-ROONEY! BUT YOU'LL BE PAID IN SPADES– ONCE YOU SIGN THIS RELEASE FORM, NATCH!
AND THE COUNT AND RAFFERTY ARE ACTORS, TOO!
NOT THEM! MR. VON HADA LET US USE HIS HOUSE FOR FILMING– ON THE CONDITION THAT HE AND HIS SERVANT TOOK PART!
BUT THAT VAN THAT ALMOST SQUISHED US–
WAS PART OF THE PLAN, TOO... TO STOP SOMEBODY NEAR THE HADA HOUSE! YOU JUST BLUNDERED BY!
AND IF WE GOT HIT?
YOU'D SURVIVE! THE VAN'S BODY WAS MADE OUT OF CARDBOARD! YOUR CAR MIGHTA TAKEN A FEW SCRATCHES... THAT'S ALL!
SAYONARA, DUCKS! SO LONG, COUNT!
HAPPY HALLOWEEN!

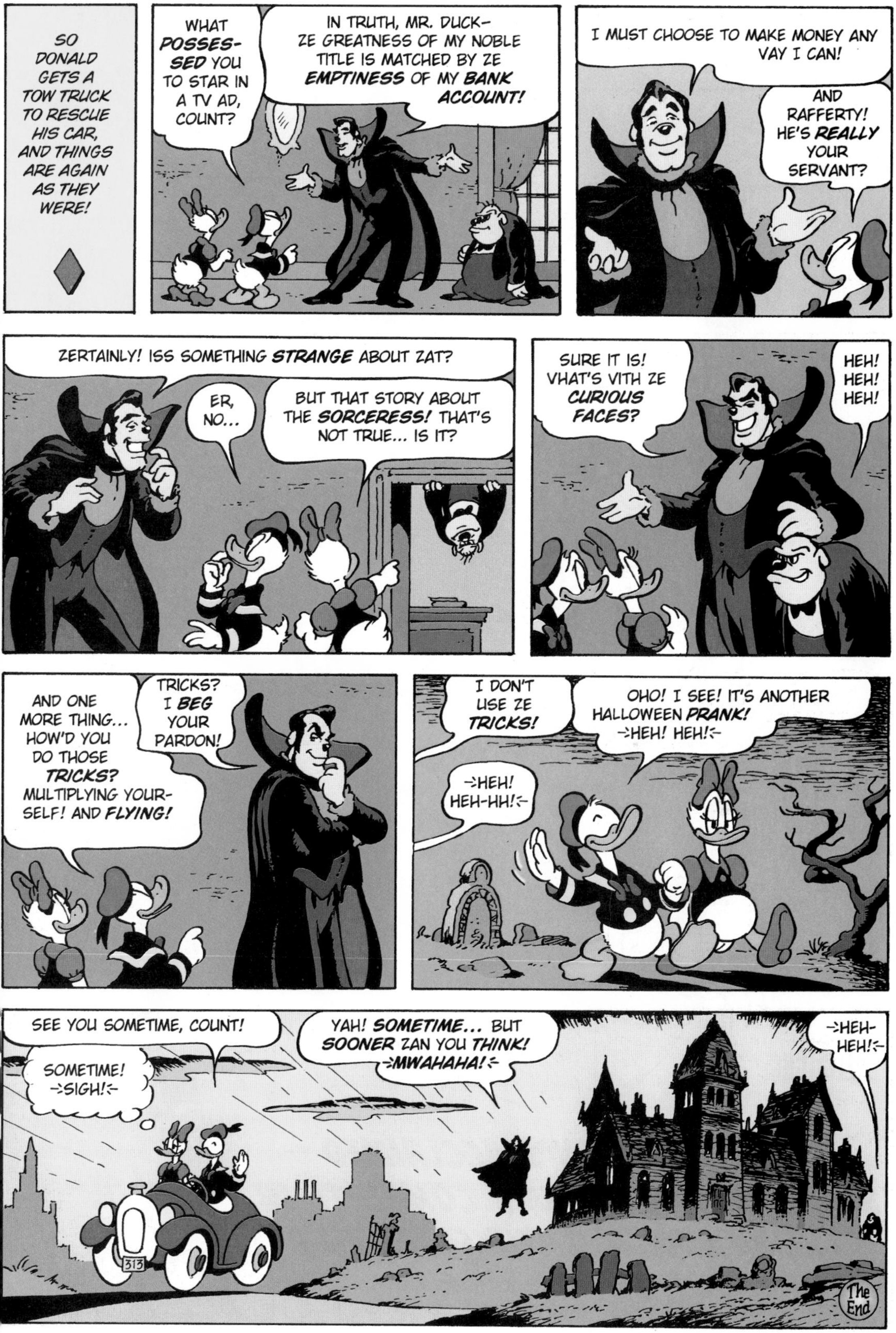

SO DONALD GETS A TOW TRUCK TO RESCUE HIS CAR, AND THINGS ARE AGAIN AS THEY WERE!
WHAT POSSES-SED YOU TO STAR IN A TV AD, COUNT?
IN TRUTH, MR. DUCK— ZE GREATNESS OF MY NOBLE TITLE IS MATCHED BY ZE EMPTINESS OF MY BANK ACCOUNT!
I MUST CHOOSE TO MAKE MONEY ANY VAY I CAN!
AND RAFFERTY! HE'S REALLY YOUR SERVANT?
ZERTAINLY! ISS SOMETHING STRANGE ABOUT ZAT?
ER, NO...
BUT THAT STORY ABOUT THE SORCERESS! THAT'S NOT TRUE... IS IT?
SURE IT IS! VHAT'S VITH ZE CURIOUS FACES?
HEH! HEH! HEH!
AND ONE MORE THING... HOW'D YOU DO THOSE TRICKS? MULTIPLYING YOUR-SELF! AND FLYING!
TRICKS? I BEG YOUR PARDON!
I DON'T USE ZE TRICKS!
OHO! I SEE! IT'S ANOTHER HALLOWEEN PRANK! ~HEH! HEH!~
~HEH! HEH-HH!~
SEE YOU SOMETIME, COUNT!
SOMETIME! ~SIGH!~
YAH! SOMETIME... BUT SOONER ZAN YOU THINK! ~MWAHAHA!~
~HEH-HEH!~
313
The End

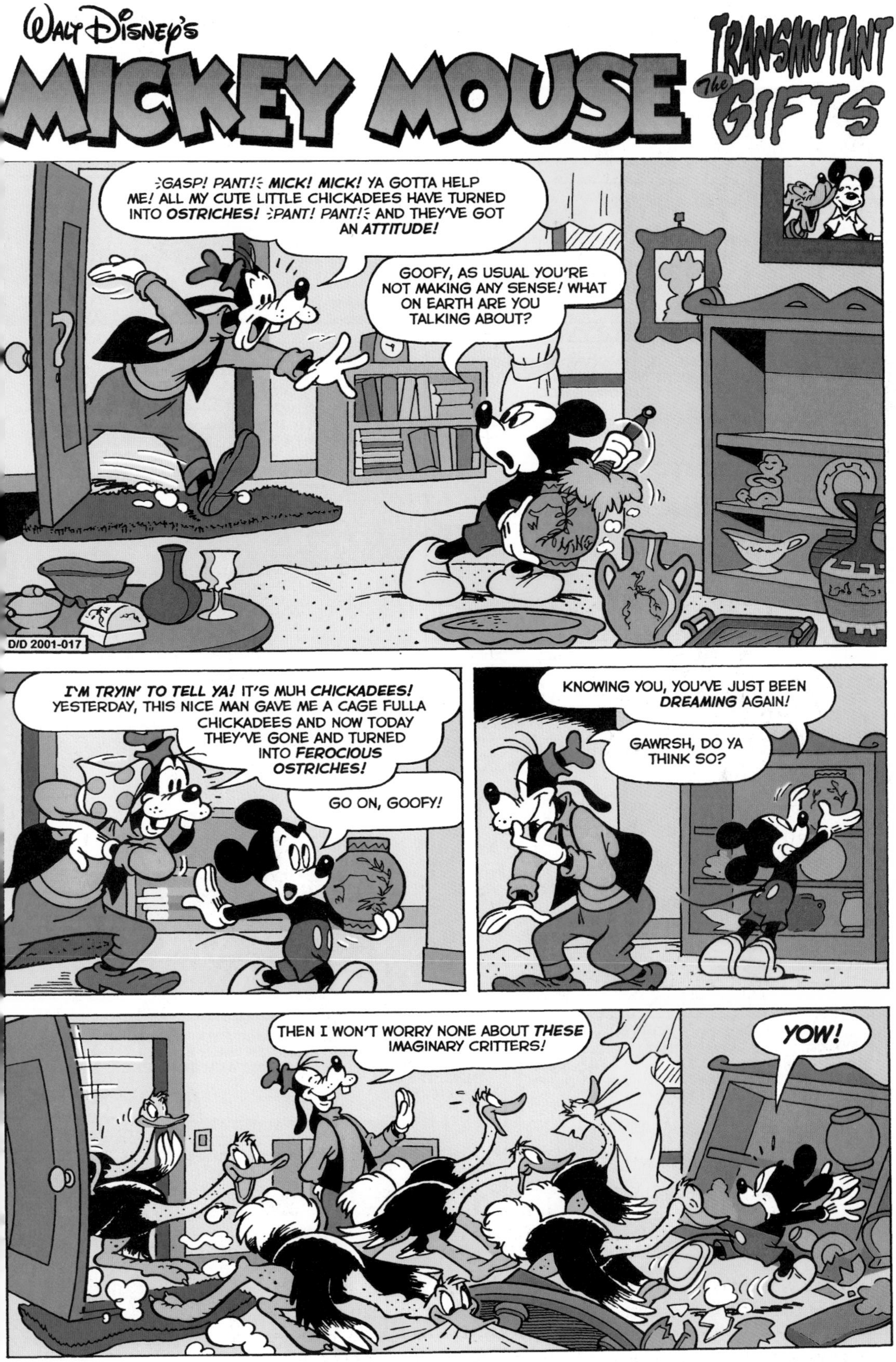

WALT DISNEY'S
MICKEY MOUSE
The TRANSMUTANT GIFTS
⁝GASP! PANT!⁝ MICK! MICK! YA GOTTA HELP ME! ALL MY CUTE LITTLE CHICKADEES HAVE TURNED INTO OSTRICHES! ⁝PANT! PANT!⁝ AND THEY'VE GOT AN ATTITUDE!
GOOFY, AS USUAL YOU'RE NOT MAKING ANY SENSE! WHAT ON EARTH ARE YOU TALKING ABOUT?
D/D 2001-017
I'M TRYIN' TO TELL YA! IT'S MUH CHICKADEES! YESTERDAY, THIS NICE MAN GAVE ME A CAGE FULLA CHICKADEES AND NOW TODAY THEY'VE GONE AND TURNED INTO FEROCIOUS OSTRICHES!
GO ON, GOOFY!
KNOWING YOU, YOU'VE JUST BEEN DREAMING AGAIN!
GAWRSH, DO YA THINK SO?
THEN I WON'T WORRY NONE ABOUT THESE IMAGINARY CRITTERS!
YOW!

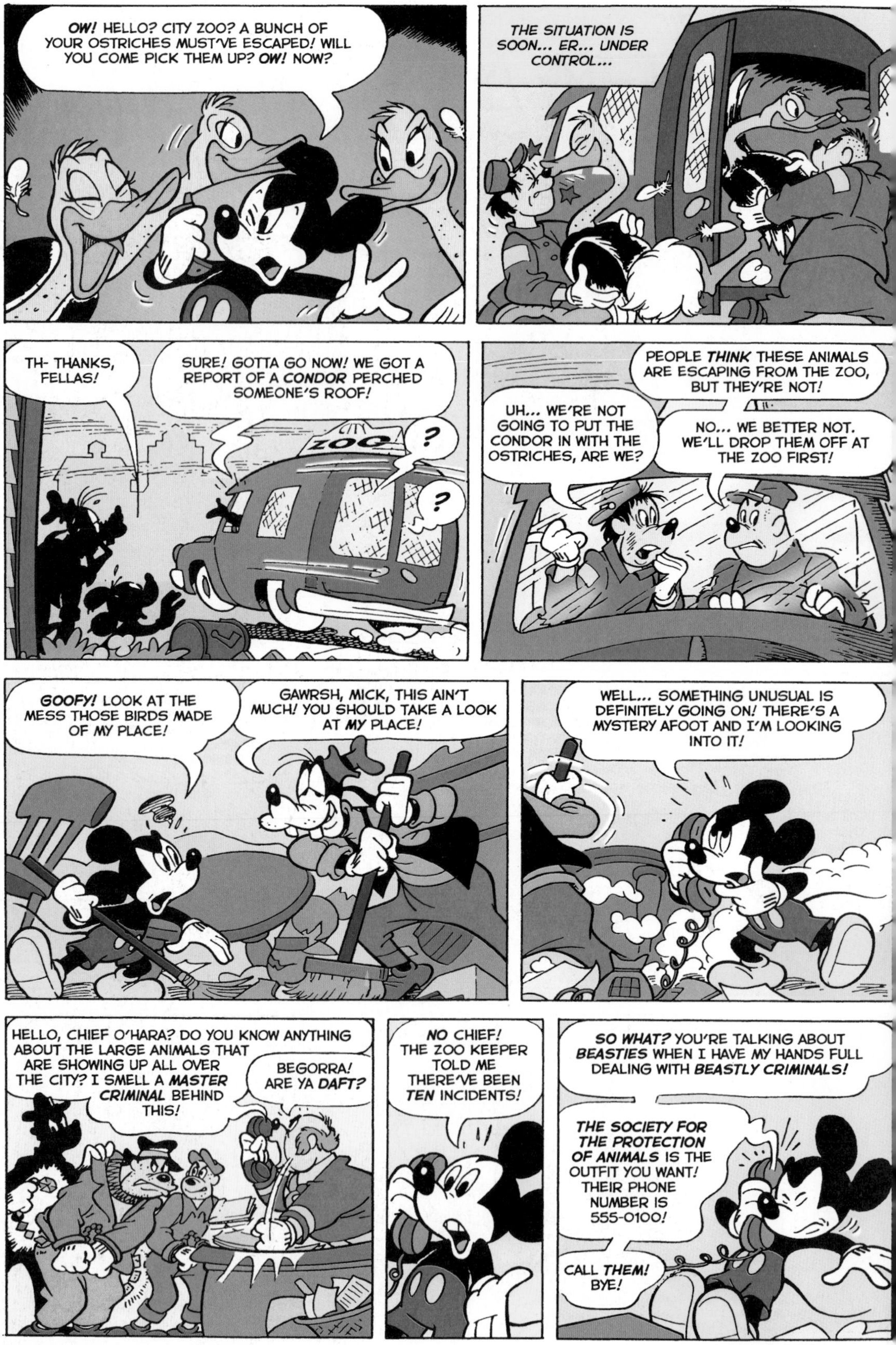
OW! HELLO? CITY ZOO? A BUNCH OF YOUR OSTRICHES MUST'VE ESCAPED! WILL YOU COME PICK THEM UP? OW! NOW?
THE SITUATION IS SOON... ER... UNDER CONTROL...
TH- THANKS, FELLAS!
SURE! GOTTA GO NOW! WE GOT A REPORT OF A CONDOR PERCHED SOMEONE'S ROOF!
CITY ZOO
?
?
PEOPLE THINK THESE ANIMALS ARE ESCAPING FROM THE ZOO, BUT THEY'RE NOT!
UH... WE'RE NOT GOING TO PUT THE CONDOR IN WITH THE OSTRICHES, ARE WE?
NO... WE BETTER NOT. WE'LL DROP THEM OFF AT THE ZOO FIRST!
GOOFY! LOOK AT THE MESS THOSE BIRDS MADE OF MY PLACE!
GAWRSH, MICK, THIS AIN'T MUCH! YOU SHOULD TAKE A LOOK AT MY PLACE!
WELL... SOMETHING UNUSUAL IS DEFINITELY GOING ON! THERE'S A MYSTERY AFOOT AND I'M LOOKING INTO IT!
HELLO, CHIEF O'HARA? DO YOU KNOW ANYTHING ABOUT THE LARGE ANIMALS THAT ARE SHOWING UP ALL OVER THE CITY? I SMELL A MASTER CRIMINAL BEHIND THIS!
BEGORRA! ARE YA DAFT?
NO CHIEF! THE ZOO KEEPER TOLD ME THERE'VE BEEN TEN INCIDENTS!
SO WHAT? YOU'RE TALKING ABOUT BEASTIES WHEN I HAVE MY HANDS FULL DEALING WITH BEASTLY CRIMINALS!
THE SOCIETY FOR THE PROTECTION OF ANIMALS IS THE OUTFIT YOU WANT! THEIR PHONE NUMBER IS 555-0100!
CALL THEM! BYE!

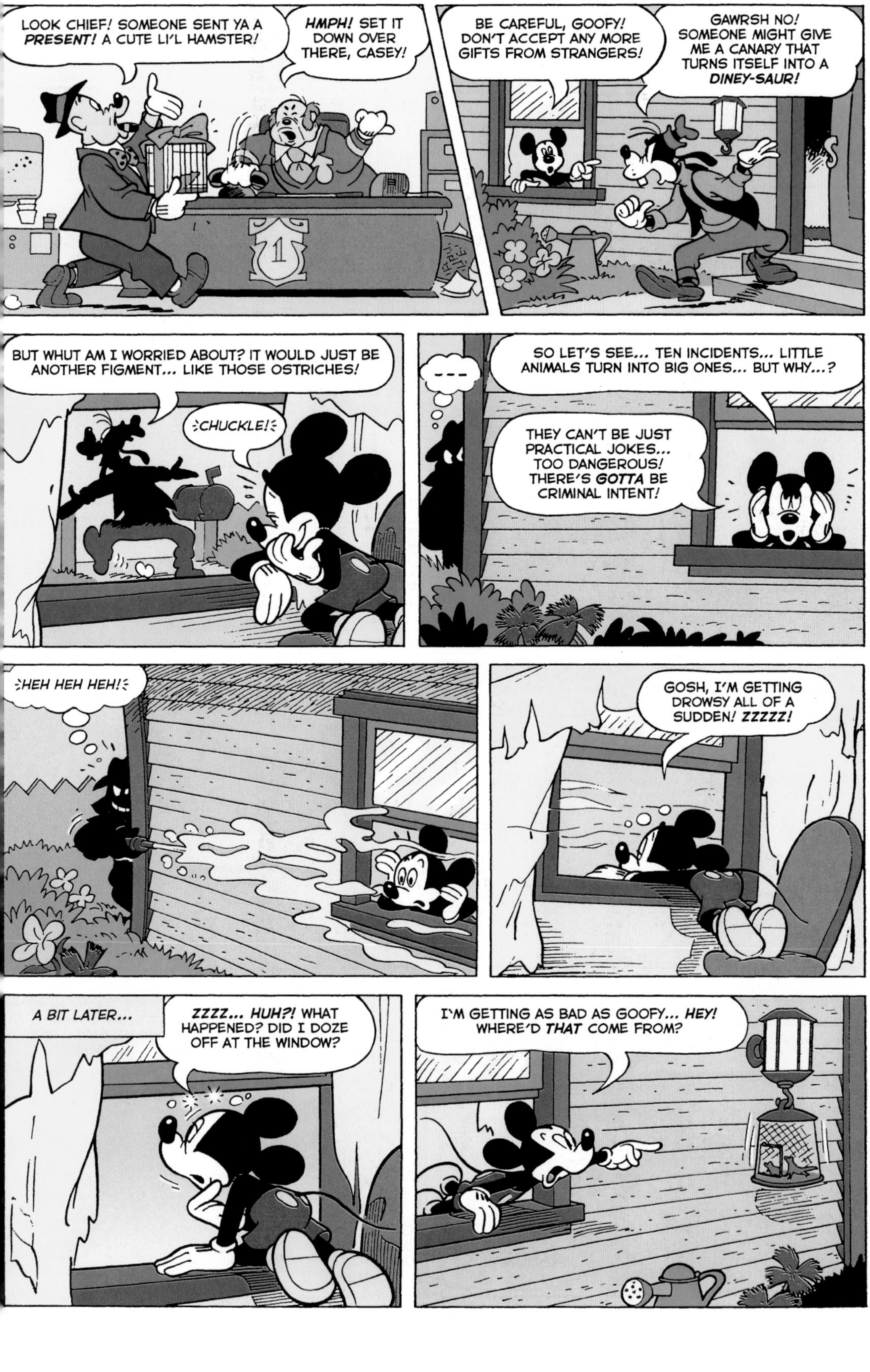

LOOK CHIEF! SOMEONE SENT YA A PRESENT! A CUTE LI'L HAMSTER!
HMPH! SET IT DOWN OVER THERE, CASEY!
1
BE CAREFUL, GOOFY! DON'T ACCEPT ANY MORE GIFTS FROM STRANGERS!
GAWRSH NO! SOMEONE MIGHT GIVE ME A CANARY THAT TURNS ITSELF INTO A DINEY-SAUR!
BUT WHUT AM I WORRIED ABOUT? IT WOULD JUST BE ANOTHER FIGMENT... LIKE THOSE OSTRICHES!
CHUCKLE!

SO LET'S SEE... TEN INCIDENTS... LITTLE ANIMALS TURN INTO BIG ONES... BUT WHY...?
THEY CAN'T BE JUST PRACTICAL JOKES... TOO DANGEROUS! THERE'S GOTTA BE CRIMINAL INTENT!
HEH HEH HEH!
GOSH, I'M GETTING DROWSY ALL OF A SUDDEN! ZZZZZ!
A BIT LATER...
ZZZZ... HUH?! WHAT HAPPENED? DID I DOZE OFF AT THE WINDOW?
I'M GETTING AS BAD AS GOOFY... HEY! WHERE'D THAT COME FROM?

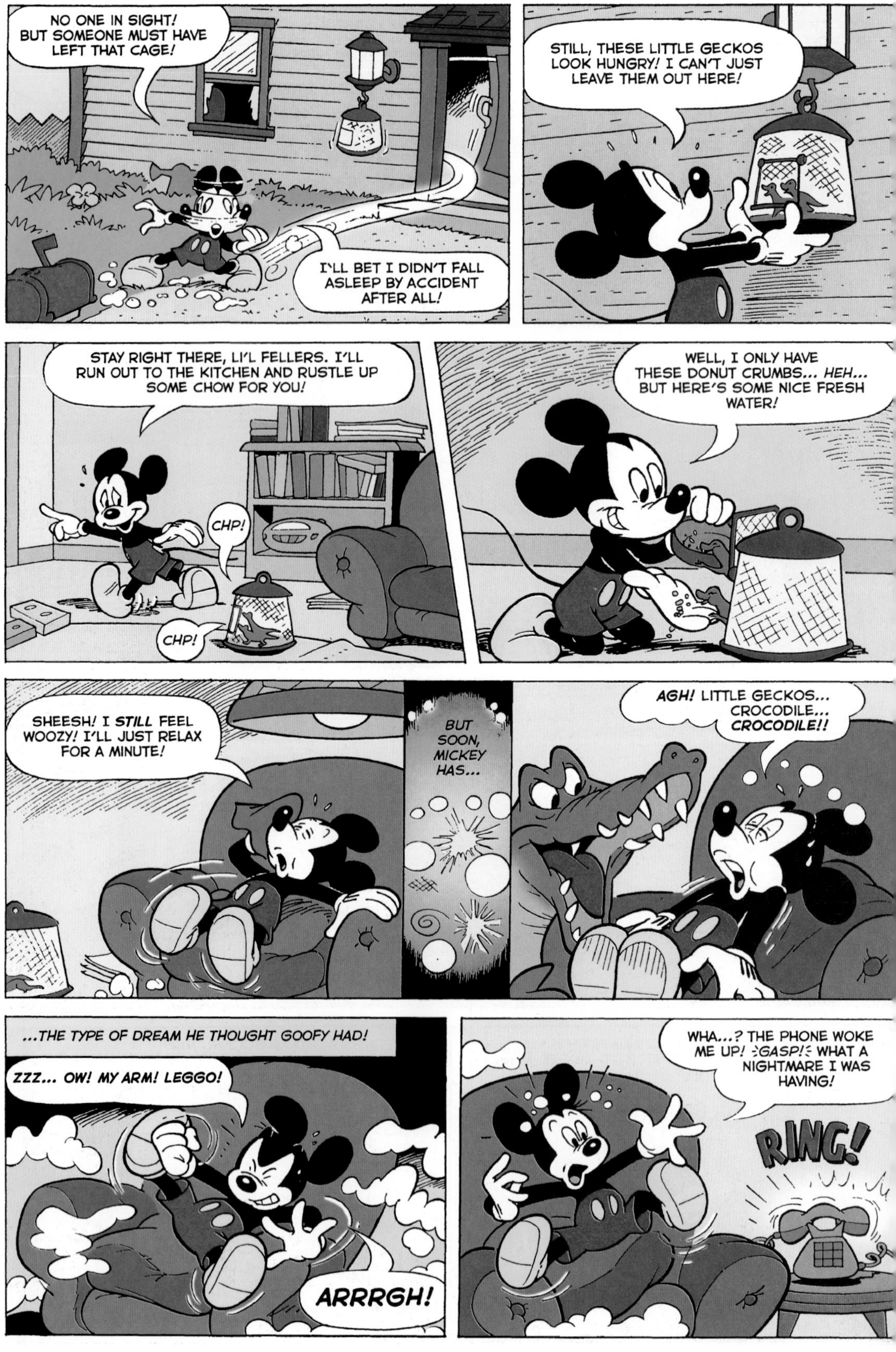
NO ONE IN SIGHT! BUT SOMEONE MUST HAVE LEFT THAT CAGE!
I'LL BET I DIDN'T FALL ASLEEP BY ACCIDENT AFTER ALL!
STILL, THESE LITTLE GECKOS LOOK HUNGRY! I CAN'T JUST LEAVE THEM OUT HERE!
STAY RIGHT THERE, LI'L FELLERS. I'LL RUN OUT TO THE KITCHEN AND RUSTLE UP SOME CHOW FOR YOU!
CHP!
CHP!
WELL, I ONLY HAVE THESE DONUT CRUMBS... HEH... BUT HERE'S SOME NICE FRESH WATER!
SHEESH! I STILL FEEL WOOZY! I'LL JUST RELAX FOR A MINUTE!
BUT SOON, MICKEY HAS...
AGH! LITTLE GECKOS... CROCODILE... CROCODILE!!
...THE TYPE OF DREAM HE THOUGHT GOOFY HAD!
ZZZ... OW! MY ARM! LEGGO!
ARRRGH!
WHA...? THE PHONE WOKE ME UP! GASP! WHAT A NIGHTMARE I WAS HAVING!
RING!

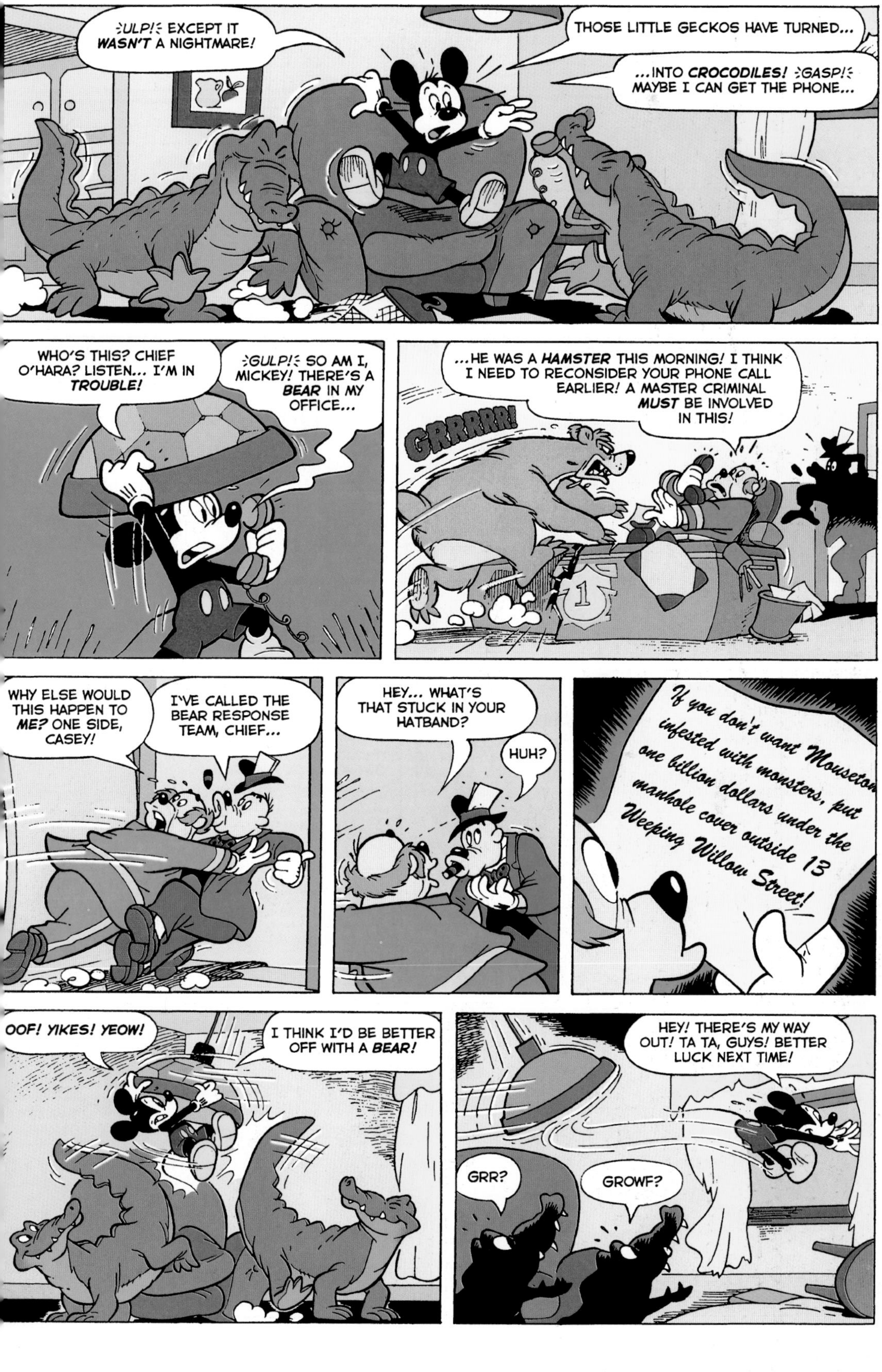

:ULP!: EXCEPT IT WASN'T A NIGHTMARE!
THOSE LITTLE GECKOS HAVE TURNED...
...INTO CROCODILES! :GASP!: MAYBE I CAN GET THE PHONE...
WHO'S THIS? CHIEF O'HARA? LISTEN... I'M IN TROUBLE!
:GULP!: SO AM I, MICKEY! THERE'S A BEAR IN MY OFFICE...
...HE WAS A HAMSTER THIS MORNING! I THINK I NEED TO RECONSIDER YOUR PHONE CALL EARLIER! A MASTER CRIMINAL MUST BE INVOLVED IN THIS!
GRRRRR!
WHY ELSE WOULD THIS HAPPEN TO ME? ONE SIDE, CASEY!
I'VE CALLED THE BEAR RESPONSE TEAM, CHIEF...
HEY... WHAT'S THAT STUCK IN YOUR HATBAND?
HUH?
If you don't want Mouseton infested with monsters, put one billion dollars under the manhole cover outside 13 Weeping Willow Street!
OOF! YIKES! YEOW!
I THINK I'D BE BETTER OFF WITH A BEAR!
HEY! THERE'S MY WAY OUT! TA TA, GUYS! BETTER LUCK NEXT TIME!
GRR?
GROWF?

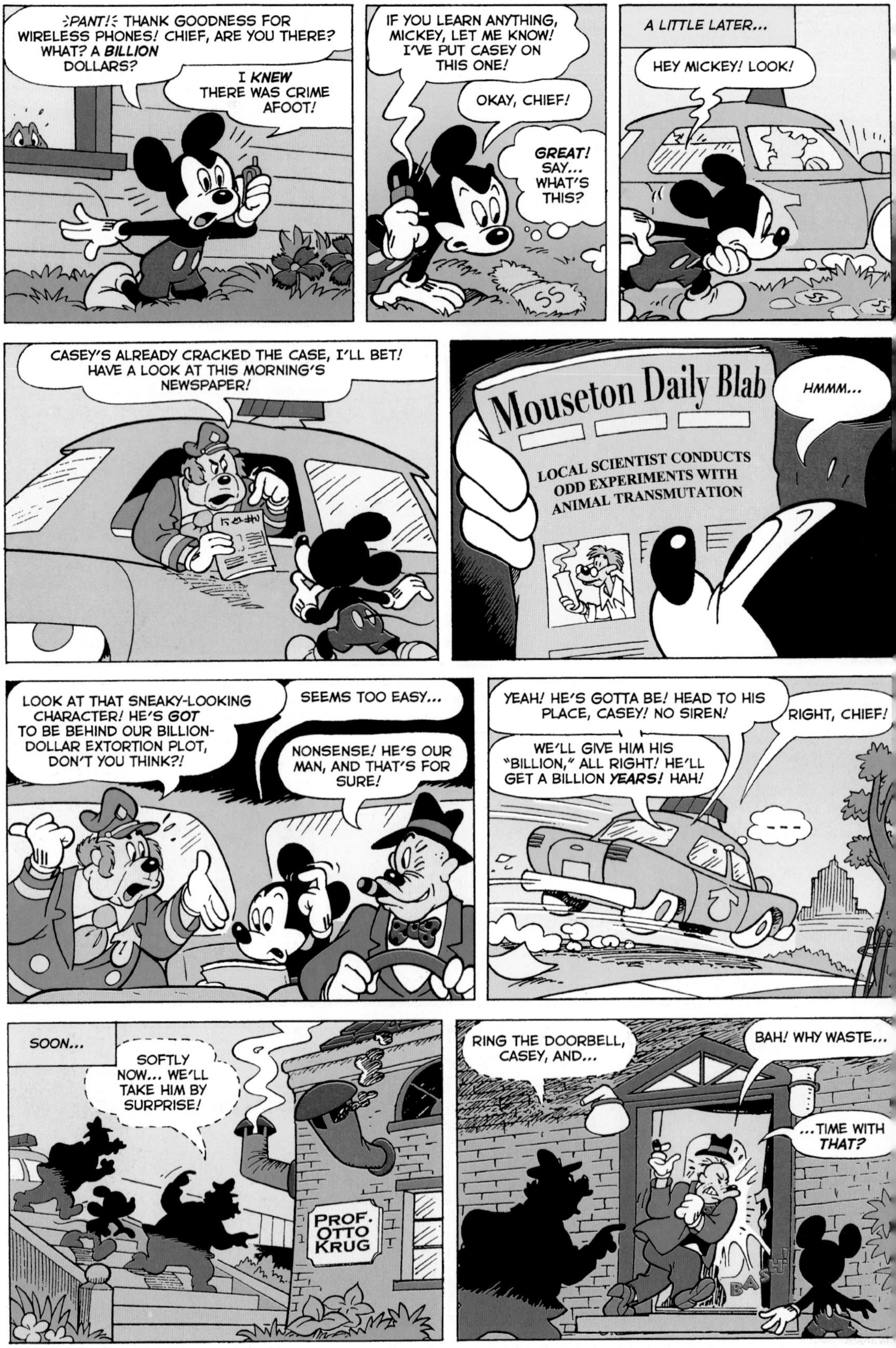

PANT! THANK GOODNESS FOR WIRELESS PHONES! CHIEF, ARE YOU THERE? WHAT? A **BILLION** DOLLARS?
I **KNEW** THERE WAS CRIME AFOOT!
IF YOU LEARN ANYTHING, MICKEY, LET ME KNOW! I'VE PUT CASEY ON THIS ONE!
OKAY, CHIEF!
GREAT! SAY... WHAT'S THIS?
A LITTLE LATER...
HEY MICKEY! LOOK!
CASEY'S ALREADY CRACKED THE CASE, I'LL BET! HAVE A LOOK AT THIS MORNING'S NEWSPAPER!
Mouseton Daily Blab
LOCAL SCIENTIST CONDUCTS ODD EXPERIMENTS WITH ANIMAL TRANSMUTATION
HMMM...
LOOK AT THAT SNEAKY-LOOKING CHARACTER! HE'S **GOT** TO BE BEHIND OUR BILLION-DOLLAR EXTORTION PLOT, DON'T YOU THINK?!
SEEMS TOO EASY...
NONSENSE! HE'S OUR MAN, AND THAT'S FOR SURE!
YEAH! HE'S GOTTA BE! HEAD TO HIS PLACE, CASEY! NO SIREN!
WE'LL GIVE HIM HIS "BILLION," ALL RIGHT! HE'LL GET A BILLION **YEARS!** HAH!
RIGHT, CHIEF!
SOON...
SOFTLY NOW... WE'LL TAKE HIM BY SURPRISE!
PROF. OTTO KRUG
RING THE DOORBELL, CASEY, AND...
BAH! WHY WASTE...
...TIME WITH **THAT?**
BASH!

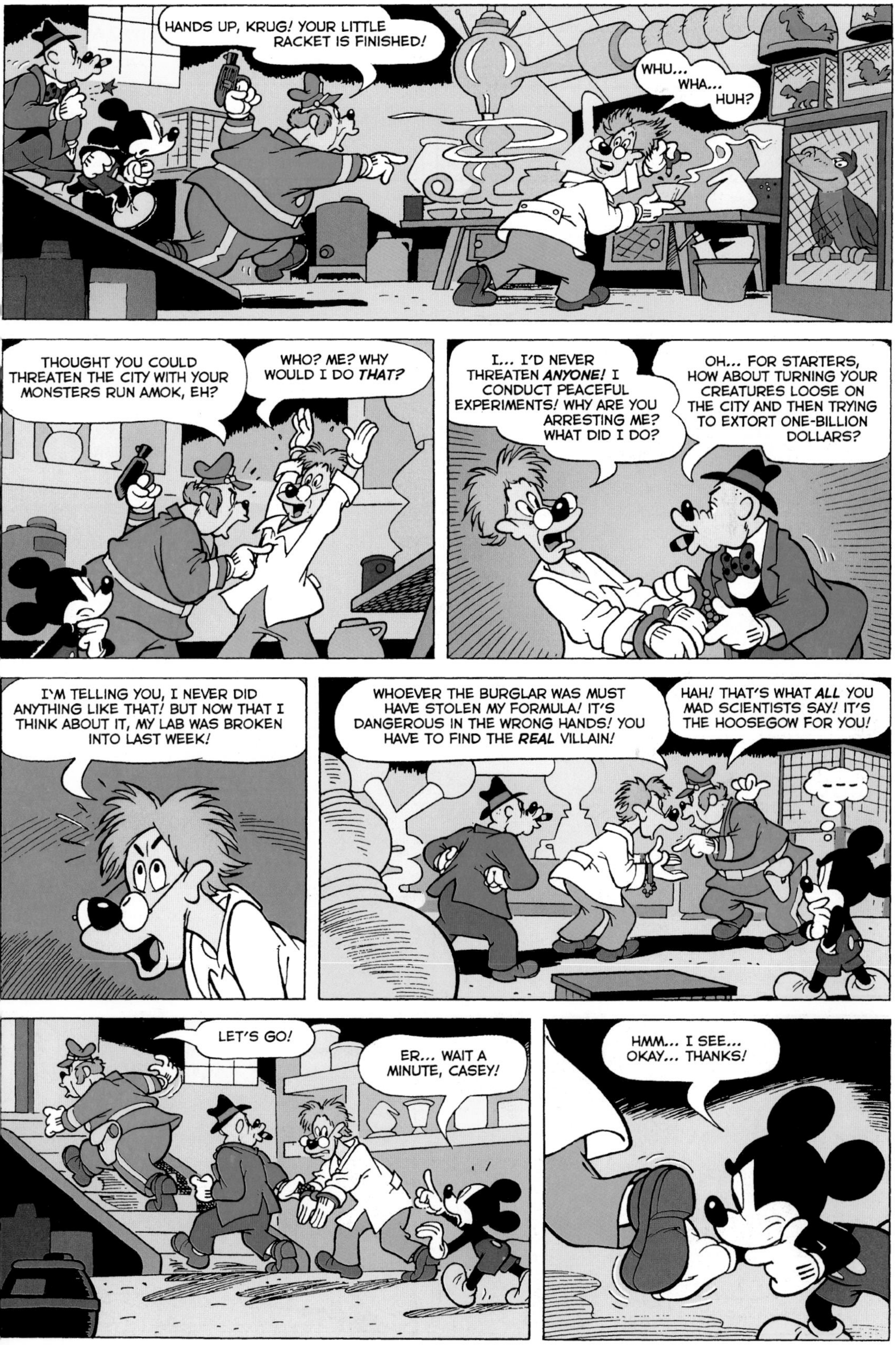
HANDS UP, KRUG! YOUR LITTLE RACKET IS FINISHED!
WHU... WHA... HUH?
THOUGHT YOU COULD THREATEN THE CITY WITH YOUR MONSTERS RUN AMOK, EH?
WHO? ME? WHY WOULD I DO THAT?
I... I'D NEVER THREATEN ANYONE! I CONDUCT PEACEFUL EXPERIMENTS! WHY ARE YOU ARRESTING ME? WHAT DID I DO?
OH... FOR STARTERS, HOW ABOUT TURNING YOUR CREATURES LOOSE ON THE CITY AND THEN TRYING TO EXTORT ONE-BILLION DOLLARS?
I'M TELLING YOU, I NEVER DID ANYTHING LIKE THAT! BUT NOW THAT I THINK ABOUT IT, MY LAB WAS BROKEN INTO LAST WEEK!
WHOEVER THE BURGLAR WAS MUST HAVE STOLEN MY FORMULA! IT'S DANGEROUS IN THE WRONG HANDS! YOU HAVE TO FIND THE REAL VILLAIN!
HAH! THAT'S WHAT ALL YOU MAD SCIENTISTS SAY! IT'S THE HOOSEGOW FOR YOU!
LET'S GO!
ER... WAIT A MINUTE, CASEY!
HMM... I SEE... OKAY... THANKS!

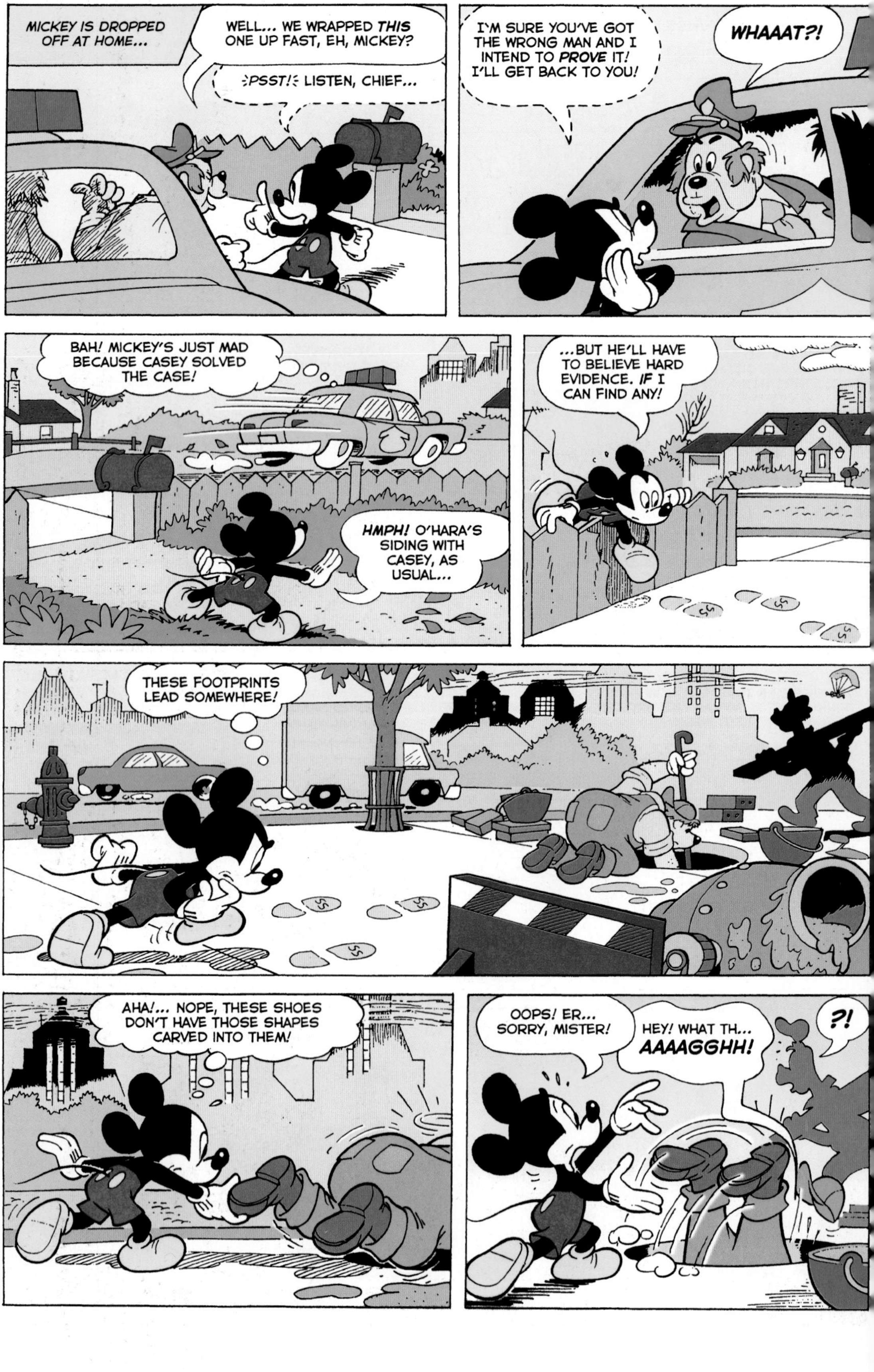
MICKEY IS DROPPED OFF AT HOME...
WELL... WE WRAPPED THIS ONE UP FAST, EH, MICKEY?
PSST! LISTEN, CHIEF...
I'M SURE YOU'VE GOT THE WRONG MAN AND I INTEND TO PROVE IT! I'LL GET BACK TO YOU!
WHAAAT?!
BAH! MICKEY'S JUST MAD BECAUSE CASEY SOLVED THE CASE!
HMPH! O'HARA'S SIDING WITH CASEY, AS USUAL...
...BUT HE'LL HAVE TO BELIEVE HARD EVIDENCE. IF I CAN FIND ANY!
THESE FOOTPRINTS LEAD SOMEWHERE!
AHA!... NOPE, THESE SHOES DON'T HAVE THOSE SHAPES CARVED INTO THEM!
OOPS! ER... SORRY, MISTER!
HEY! WHAT TH... AAAAGGHH!
?!

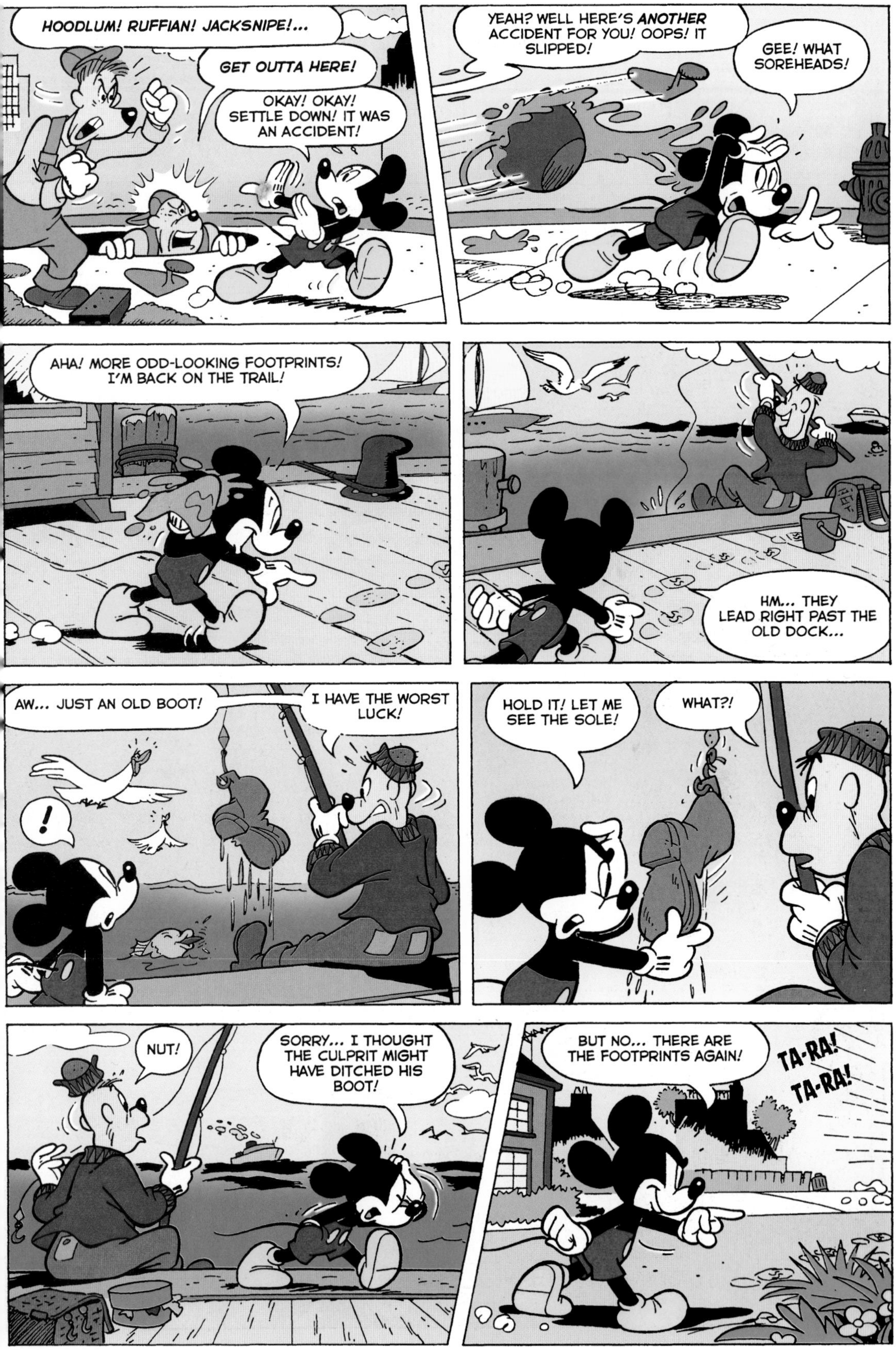
HOODLUM! RUFFIAN! JACKSNIPE!...
GET OUTTA HERE!
OKAY! OKAY! SETTLE DOWN! IT WAS AN ACCIDENT!
YEAH? WELL HERE'S ANOTHER ACCIDENT FOR YOU! OOPS! IT SLIPPED!
GEE! WHAT SOREHEADS!
AHA! MORE ODD-LOOKING FOOTPRINTS! I'M BACK ON THE TRAIL!
HM... THEY LEAD RIGHT PAST THE OLD DOCK...
AW... JUST AN OLD BOOT!
I HAVE THE WORST LUCK!
!
HOLD IT! LET ME SEE THE SOLE!
WHAT?!
NUT!
SORRY... I THOUGHT THE CULPRIT MIGHT HAVE DITCHED HIS BOOT!
BUT NO... THERE ARE THE FOOTPRINTS AGAIN!
TA-RA!
TA-RA!

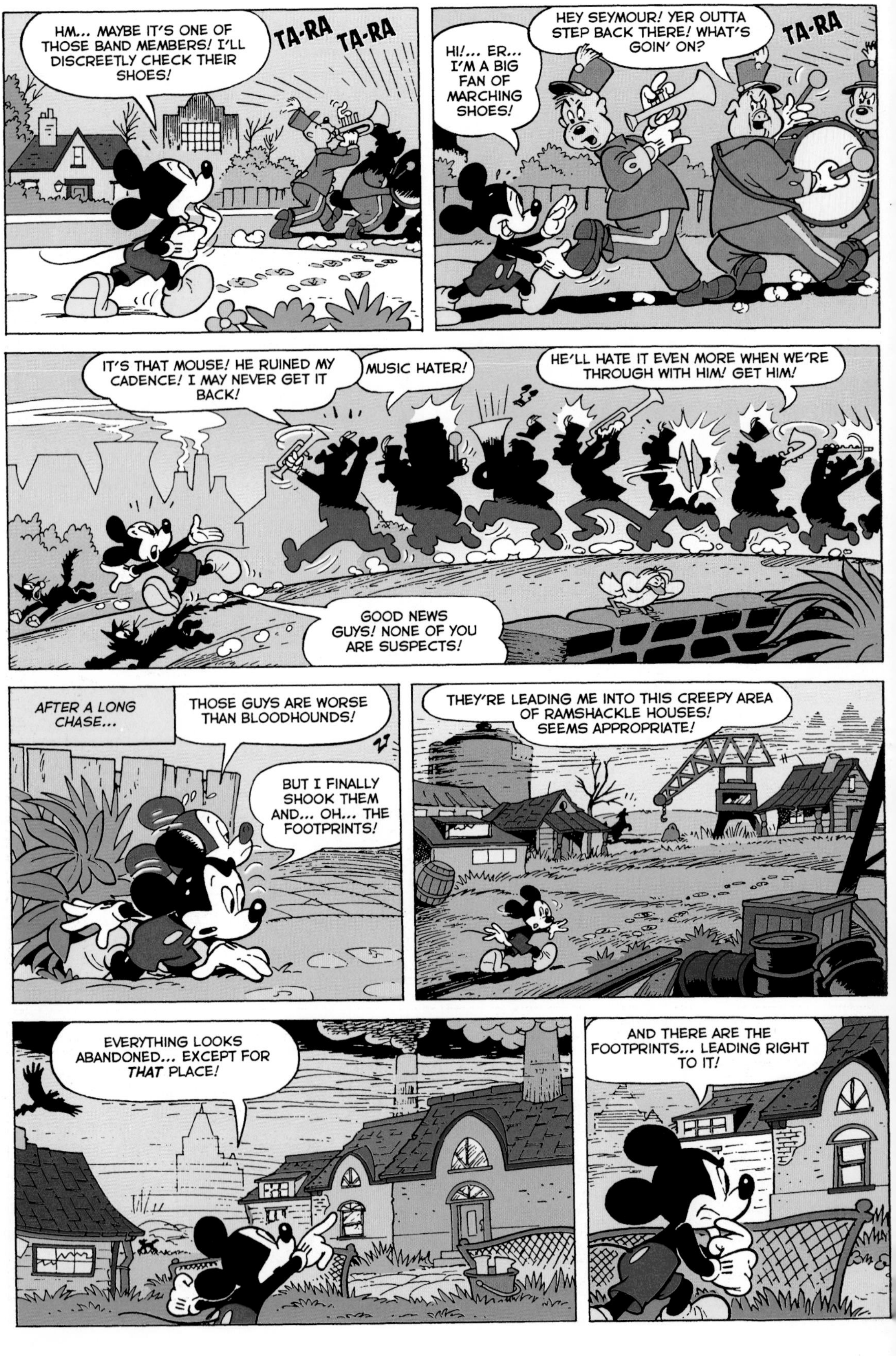
HM... MAYBE IT'S ONE OF THOSE BAND MEMBERS! I'LL DISCREETLY CHECK THEIR SHOES!
TA-RA TA-RA
HEY SEYMOUR! YER OUTTA STEP BACK THERE! WHAT'S GOIN' ON?
HI!... ER... I'M A BIG FAN OF MARCHING SHOES!
TA-RA
IT'S THAT MOUSE! HE RUINED MY CADENCE! I MAY NEVER GET IT BACK!
MUSIC HATER!
HE'LL HATE IT EVEN MORE WHEN WE'RE THROUGH WITH HIM! GET HIM!
GOOD NEWS GUYS! NONE OF YOU ARE SUSPECTS!
AFTER A LONG CHASE...
THOSE GUYS ARE WORSE THAN BLOODHOUNDS!
BUT I FINALLY SHOOK THEM AND... OH... THE FOOTPRINTS!
THEY'RE LEADING ME INTO THIS CREEPY AREA OF RAMSHACKLE HOUSES! SEEMS APPROPRIATE!
EVERYTHING LOOKS ABANDONED... EXCEPT FOR *THAT* PLACE!
AND THERE ARE THE FOOTPRINTS... LEADING RIGHT TO IT!

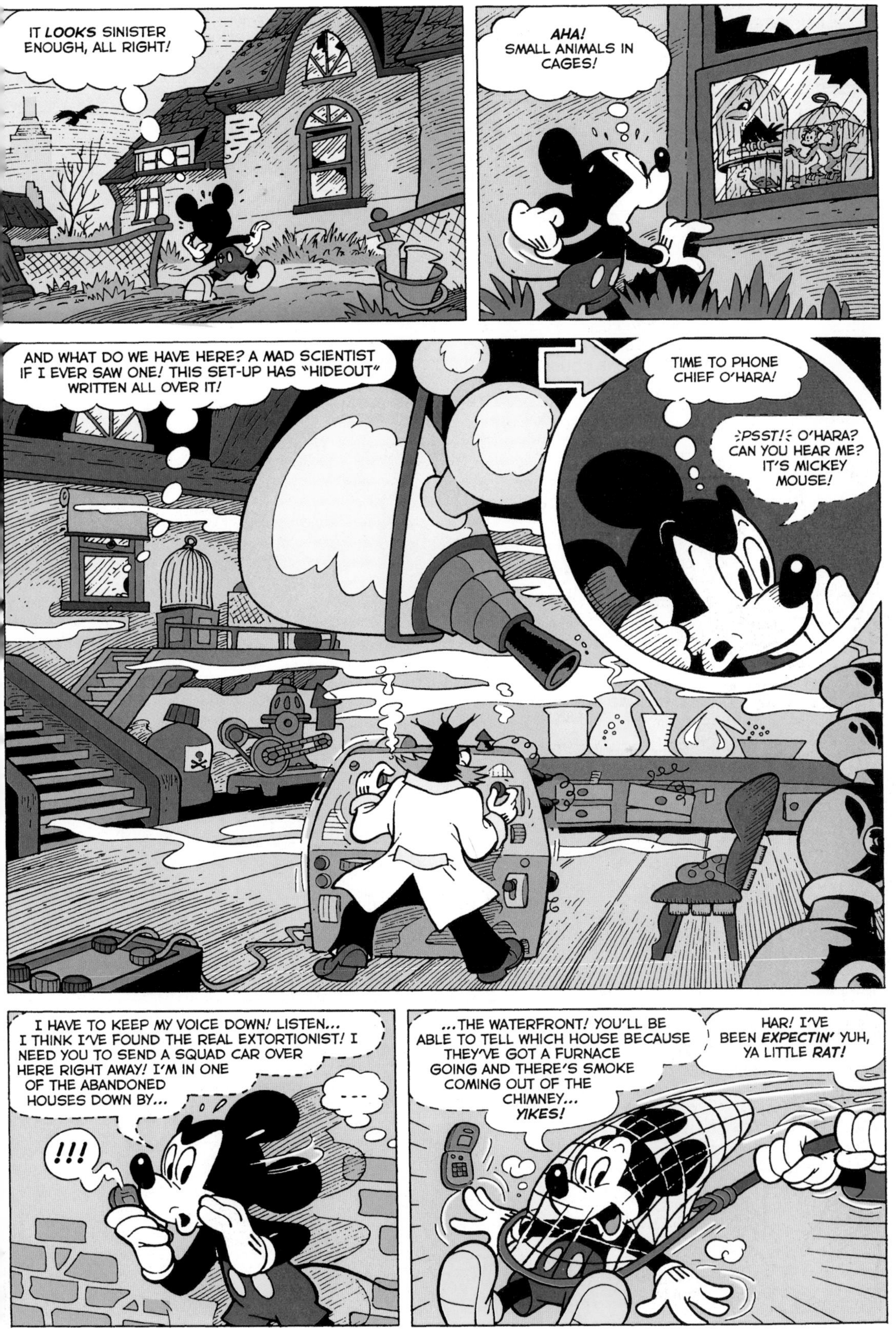
IT LOOKS SINISTER ENOUGH, ALL RIGHT!
AHA! SMALL ANIMALS IN CAGES!
AND WHAT DO WE HAVE HERE? A MAD SCIENTIST IF I EVER SAW ONE! THIS SET-UP HAS "HIDEOUT" WRITTEN ALL OVER IT!
TIME TO PHONE CHIEF O'HARA!
PSST! O'HARA? CAN YOU HEAR ME? IT'S MICKEY MOUSE!
I HAVE TO KEEP MY VOICE DOWN! LISTEN... I THINK I'VE FOUND THE REAL EXTORTIONIST! I NEED YOU TO SEND A SQUAD CAR OVER HERE RIGHT AWAY! I'M IN ONE OF THE ABANDONED HOUSES DOWN BY...

!!!
...THE WATERFRONT! YOU'LL BE ABLE TO TELL WHICH HOUSE BECAUSE THEY'VE GOT A FURNACE GOING AND THERE'S SMOKE COMING OUT OF THE CHIMNEY... YIKES!
HAR! I'VE BEEN EXPECTIN' YUH, YA LITTLE RAT!

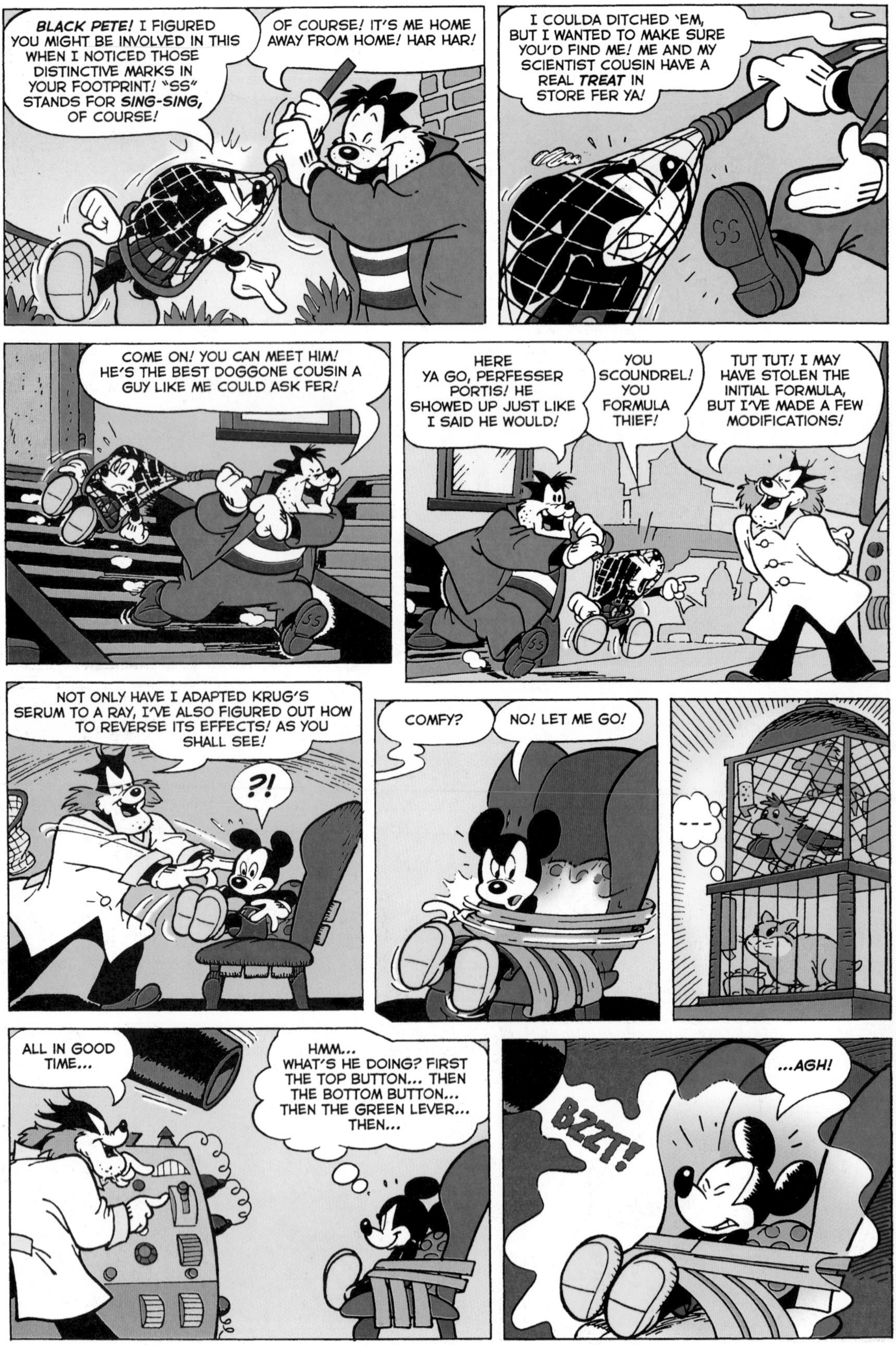
BLACK PETE! I FIGURED YOU MIGHT BE INVOLVED IN THIS WHEN I NOTICED THOSE DISTINCTIVE MARKS IN YOUR FOOTPRINT! "SS" STANDS FOR SING-SING, OF COURSE!
OF COURSE! IT'S ME HOME AWAY FROM HOME! HAR HAR!
I COULDA DITCHED 'EM, BUT I WANTED TO MAKE SURE YOU'D FIND ME! ME AND MY SCIENTIST COUSIN HAVE A REAL TREAT IN STORE FER YA!
COME ON! YOU CAN MEET HIM! HE'S THE BEST DOGGONE COUSIN A GUY LIKE ME COULD ASK FER!
HERE YA GO, PERFESSER PORTIS! HE SHOWED UP JUST LIKE I SAID HE WOULD!
YOU SCOUNDREL! YOU FORMULA THIEF!
TUT TUT! I MAY HAVE STOLEN THE INITIAL FORMULA, BUT I'VE MADE A FEW MODIFICATIONS!
NOT ONLY HAVE I ADAPTED KRUG'S SERUM TO A RAY, I'VE ALSO FIGURED OUT HOW TO REVERSE ITS EFFECTS! AS YOU SHALL SEE!
?!
COMFY?
NO! LET ME GO!
- - -
ALL IN GOOD TIME...
HMM... WHAT'S HE DOING? FIRST THE TOP BUTTON... THEN THE BOTTOM BUTTON... THEN THE GREEN LEVER... THEN...
BZZZT!
...AGH!

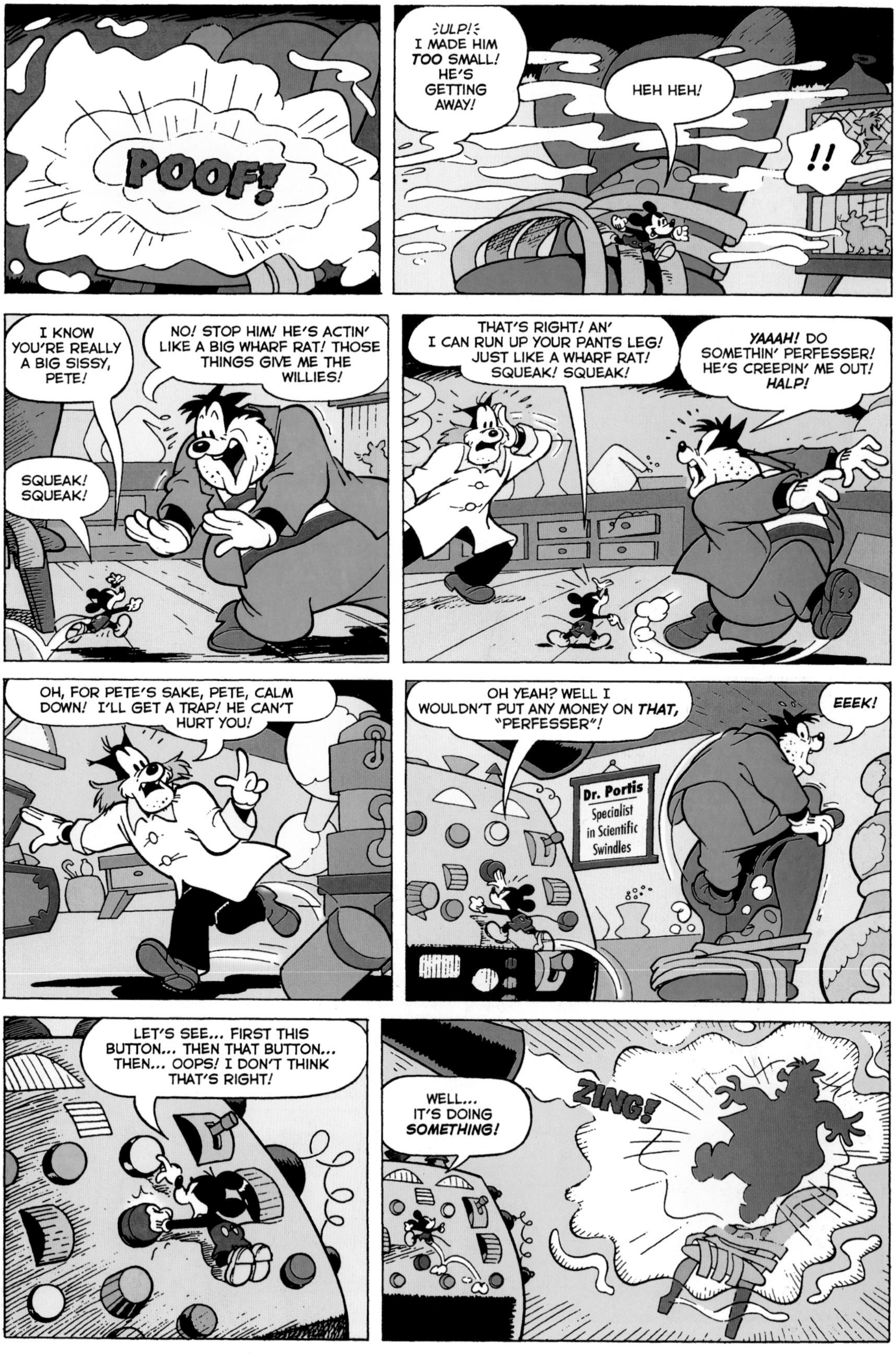
POOF!
ULP! I MADE HIM TOO SMALL! HE'S GETTING AWAY!
HEH HEH!
!!
I KNOW YOU'RE REALLY A BIG SISSY, PETE!
NO! STOP HIM! HE'S ACTIN' LIKE A BIG WHARF RAT! THOSE THINGS GIVE ME THE WILLIES!
SQUEAK! SQUEAK!
THAT'S RIGHT! AN' I CAN RUN UP YOUR PANTS LEG! JUST LIKE A WHARF RAT! SQUEAK! SQUEAK!
YAAAH! DO SOMETHIN' PERFESSER! HE'S CREEPIN' ME OUT! HALP!
OH, FOR PETE'S SAKE, PETE, CALM DOWN! I'LL GET A TRAP! HE CAN'T HURT YOU!
OH YEAH? WELL I WOULDN'T PUT ANY MONEY ON THAT, "PERFESSER"!
EEEK!
Dr. Portis
Specialist in Scientific Swindles
LET'S SEE... FIRST THIS BUTTON... THEN THAT BUTTON... THEN... OOPS! I DON'T THINK THAT'S RIGHT!
WELL... IT'S DOING SOMETHING!
ZING!

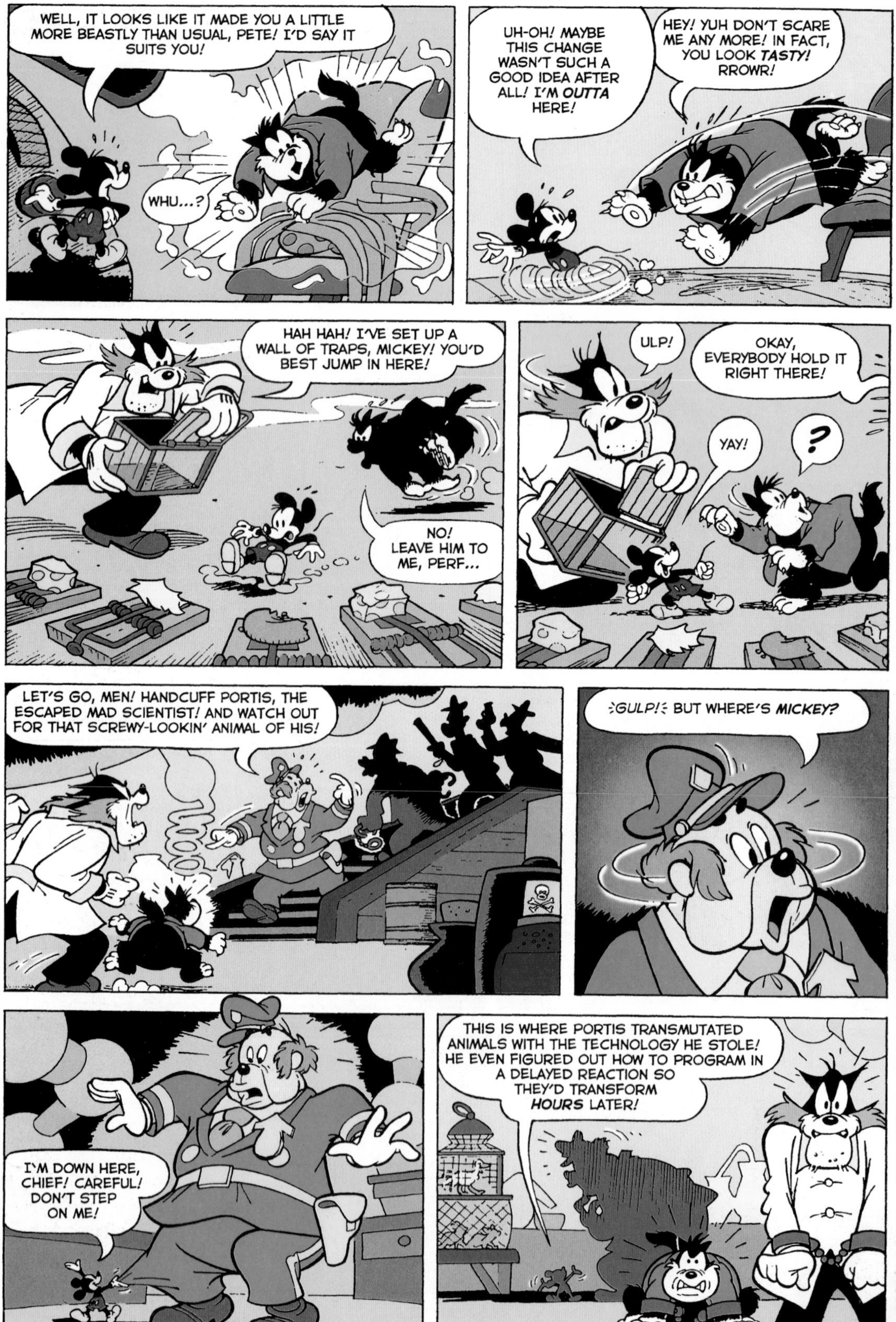

WELL, IT LOOKS LIKE IT MADE YOU A LITTLE MORE BEASTLY THAN USUAL, PETE! I'D SAY IT SUITS YOU!
WHU...?
UH-OH! MAYBE THIS CHANGE WASN'T SUCH A GOOD IDEA AFTER ALL! I'M OUTTA HERE!
HEY! YUH DON'T SCARE ME ANY MORE! IN FACT, YOU LOOK TASTY! RROWR!
HAH HAH! I'VE SET UP A WALL OF TRAPS, MICKEY! YOU'D BEST JUMP IN HERE!
NO! LEAVE HIM TO ME, PERF...
ULP!
OKAY, EVERYBODY HOLD IT RIGHT THERE!
YAY!
?
LET'S GO, MEN! HANDCUFF PORTIS, THE ESCAPED MAD SCIENTIST! AND WATCH OUT FOR THAT SCREWY-LOOKIN' ANIMAL OF HIS!
GULP! BUT WHERE'S MICKEY?
I'M DOWN HERE, CHIEF! CAREFUL! DON'T STEP ON ME!
THIS IS WHERE PORTIS TRANSMUTATED ANIMALS WITH THE TECHNOLOGY HE STOLE! HE EVEN FIGURED OUT HOW TO PROGRAM IN A DELAYED REACTION SO THEY'D TRANSFORM HOURS LATER!

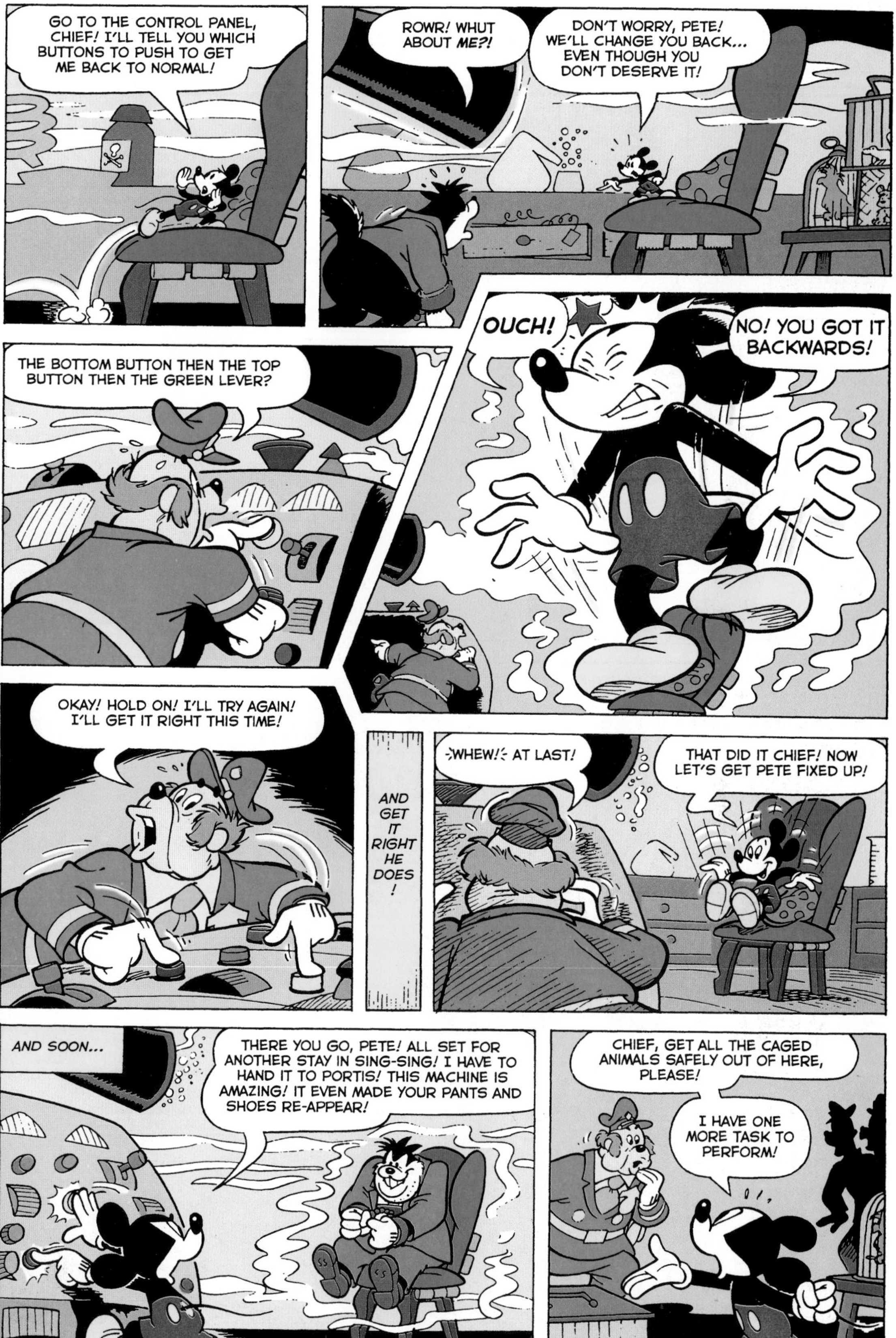
GO TO THE CONTROL PANEL, CHIEF! I'LL TELL YOU WHICH BUTTONS TO PUSH TO GET ME BACK TO NORMAL!
ROWR! WHUT ABOUT *ME?!*
DON'T WORRY, PETE! WE'LL CHANGE YOU BACK... EVEN THOUGH YOU DON'T DESERVE IT!
THE BOTTOM BUTTON THEN THE TOP BUTTON THEN THE GREEN LEVER?
OUCH!
NO! YOU GOT IT BACKWARDS!
OKAY! HOLD ON! I'LL TRY AGAIN! I'LL GET IT RIGHT THIS TIME!
AND GET IT RIGHT HE DOES!
WHEW! AT LAST!
THAT DID IT CHIEF! NOW LET'S GET PETE FIXED UP!
AND SOON...
THERE YOU GO, PETE! ALL SET FOR ANOTHER STAY IN SING-SING! I HAVE TO HAND IT TO PORTIS! THIS MACHINE IS AMAZING! IT EVEN MADE YOUR PANTS AND SHOES RE-APPEAR!
CHIEF, GET ALL THE CAGED ANIMALS SAFELY OUT OF HERE, PLEASE!
I HAVE ONE MORE TASK TO PERFORM!

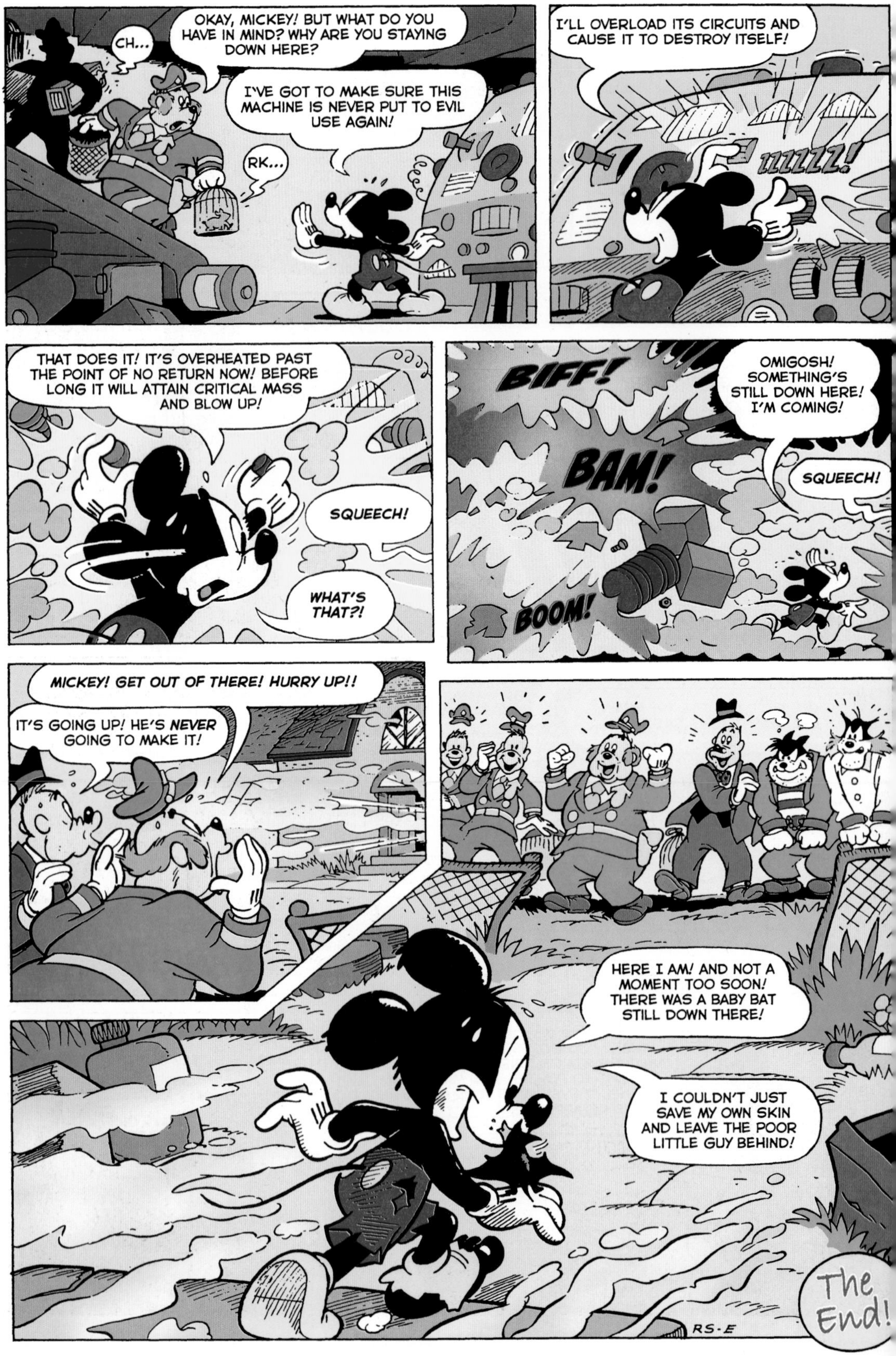

OKAY, MICKEY! BUT WHAT DO YOU HAVE IN MIND? WHY ARE YOU STAYING DOWN HERE?
CH...
I'VE GOT TO MAKE SURE THIS MACHINE IS NEVER PUT TO EVIL USE AGAIN!
RK...
I'LL OVERLOAD ITS CIRCUITS AND CAUSE IT TO DESTROY ITSELF!
ZZZZZZ!
THAT DOES IT! IT'S OVERHEATED PAST THE POINT OF NO RETURN NOW! BEFORE LONG IT WILL ATTAIN CRITICAL MASS AND BLOW UP!
SQUEECH!
WHAT'S THAT?!
BIFF!
BAM!
BOOM!
OMIGOSH! SOMETHING'S STILL DOWN HERE! I'M COMING!
SQUEECH!
MICKEY! GET OUT OF THERE! HURRY UP!!
IT'S GOING UP! HE'S NEVER GOING TO MAKE IT!
HERE I AM! AND NOT A MOMENT TOO SOON! THERE WAS A BABY BAT STILL DOWN THERE!
I COULDN'T JUST SAVE MY OWN SKIN AND LEAVE THE POOR LITTLE GUY BEHIND!
The End!
RS-E

Walt Disney's Huey, Dewey & Louie in HAPPY BIRTHDAY TIMES THREE

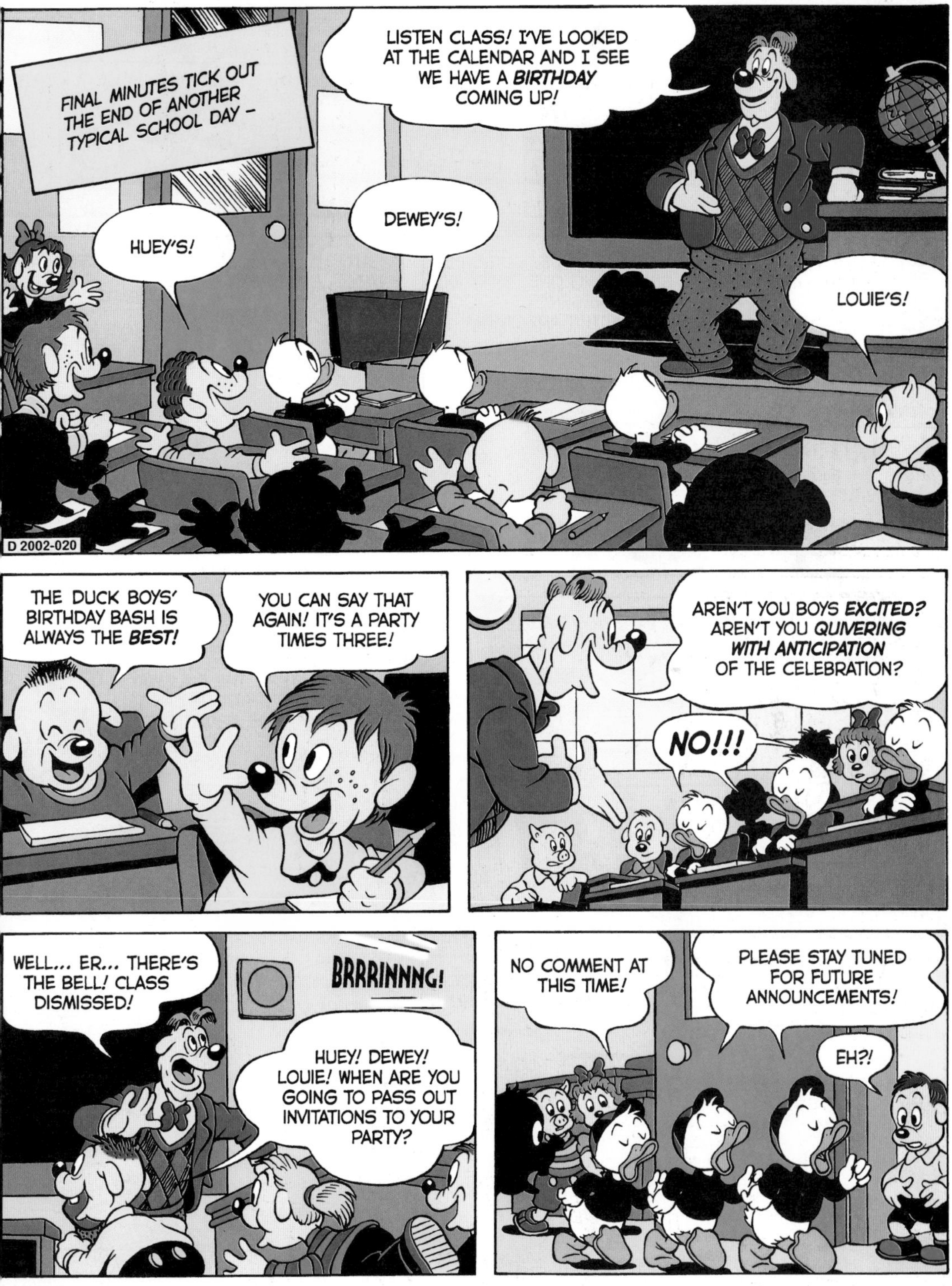

FINAL MINUTES TICK OUT THE END OF ANOTHER TYPICAL SCHOOL DAY –
LISTEN CLASS! I'VE LOOKED AT THE CALENDAR AND I SEE WE HAVE A *BIRTHDAY* COMING UP!
HUEY'S!
DEWEY'S!
LOUIE'S!
D 2002-020
THE DUCK BOYS' BIRTHDAY BASH IS ALWAYS THE *BEST!*
YOU CAN SAY THAT AGAIN! IT'S A PARTY TIMES THREE!
AREN'T YOU BOYS *EXCITED?* AREN'T YOU *QUIVERING WITH ANTICIPATION* OF THE CELEBRATION?
NO!!!
WELL... ER... THERE'S THE BELL! CLASS DISMISSED!
BRRRINNNG!
HUEY! DEWEY! LOUIE! WHEN ARE YOU GOING TO PASS OUT INVITATIONS TO YOUR PARTY?
NO COMMENT AT THIS TIME!
PLEASE STAY TUNED FOR FUTURE ANNOUNCEMENTS!
EH?!

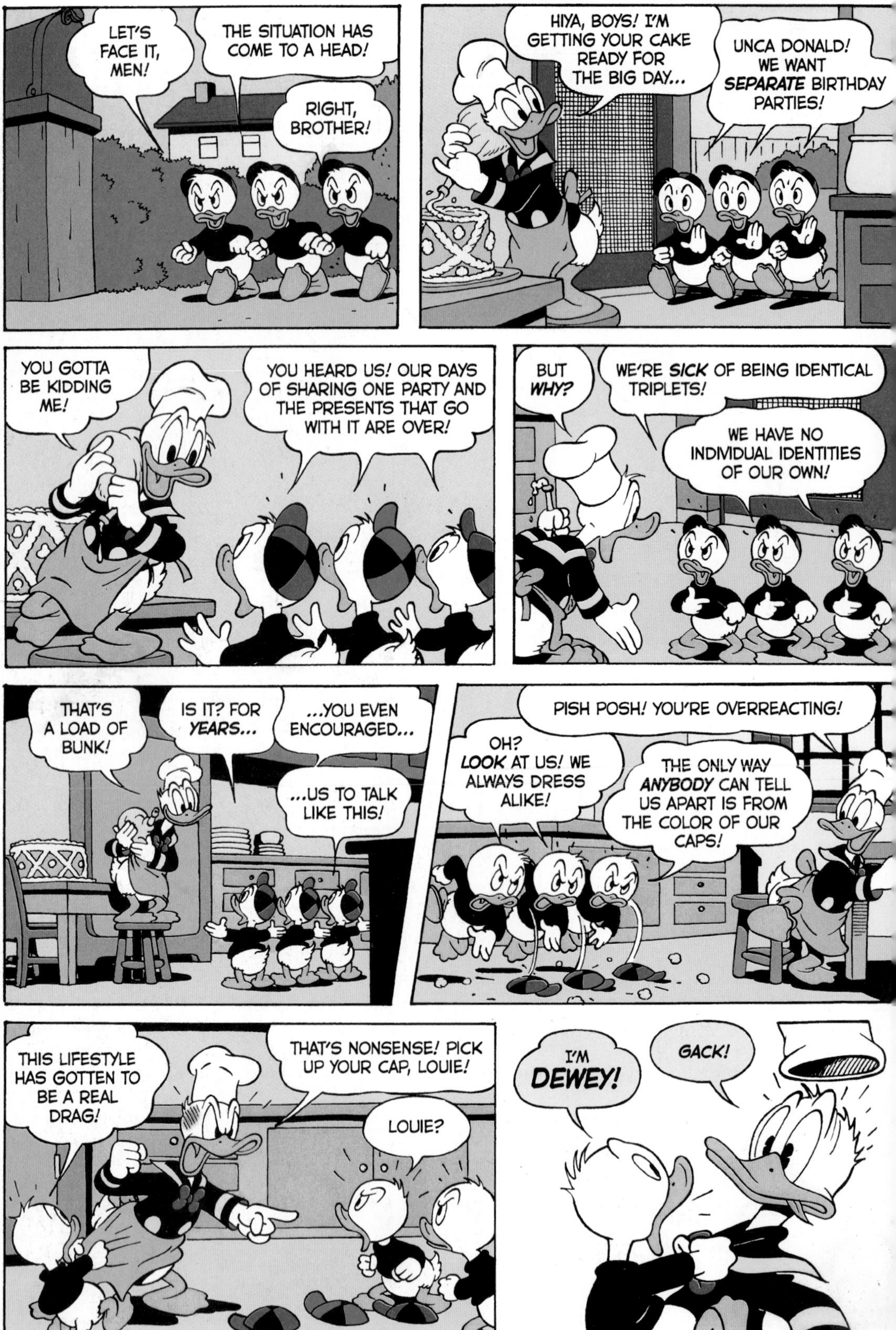

LET'S FACE IT, MEN!
THE SITUATION HAS COME TO A HEAD!
RIGHT, BROTHER!
HIYA, BOYS! I'M GETTING YOUR CAKE READY FOR THE BIG DAY...
UNCA DONALD! WE WANT *SEPARATE* BIRTHDAY PARTIES!
YOU GOTTA BE KIDDING ME!
YOU HEARD US! OUR DAYS OF SHARING ONE PARTY AND THE PRESENTS THAT GO WITH IT ARE OVER!
BUT *WHY?*
WE'RE *SICK* OF BEING IDENTICAL TRIPLETS!
WE HAVE NO INDIVIDUAL IDENTITIES OF OUR OWN!
THAT'S A LOAD OF BUNK!
IS IT? FOR *YEARS...*
...YOU EVEN ENCOURAGED...
...US TO TALK LIKE THIS!
PISH POSH! YOU'RE OVERREACTING!
OH? *LOOK* AT US! WE ALWAYS DRESS ALIKE!
THE ONLY WAY *ANYBODY* CAN TELL US APART IS FROM THE COLOR OF OUR CAPS!
THIS LIFESTYLE HAS GOTTEN TO BE A REAL DRAG!
THAT'S NONSENSE! PICK UP YOUR CAP, LOUIE!
LOUIE?
I'M *DEWEY!*
GACK!

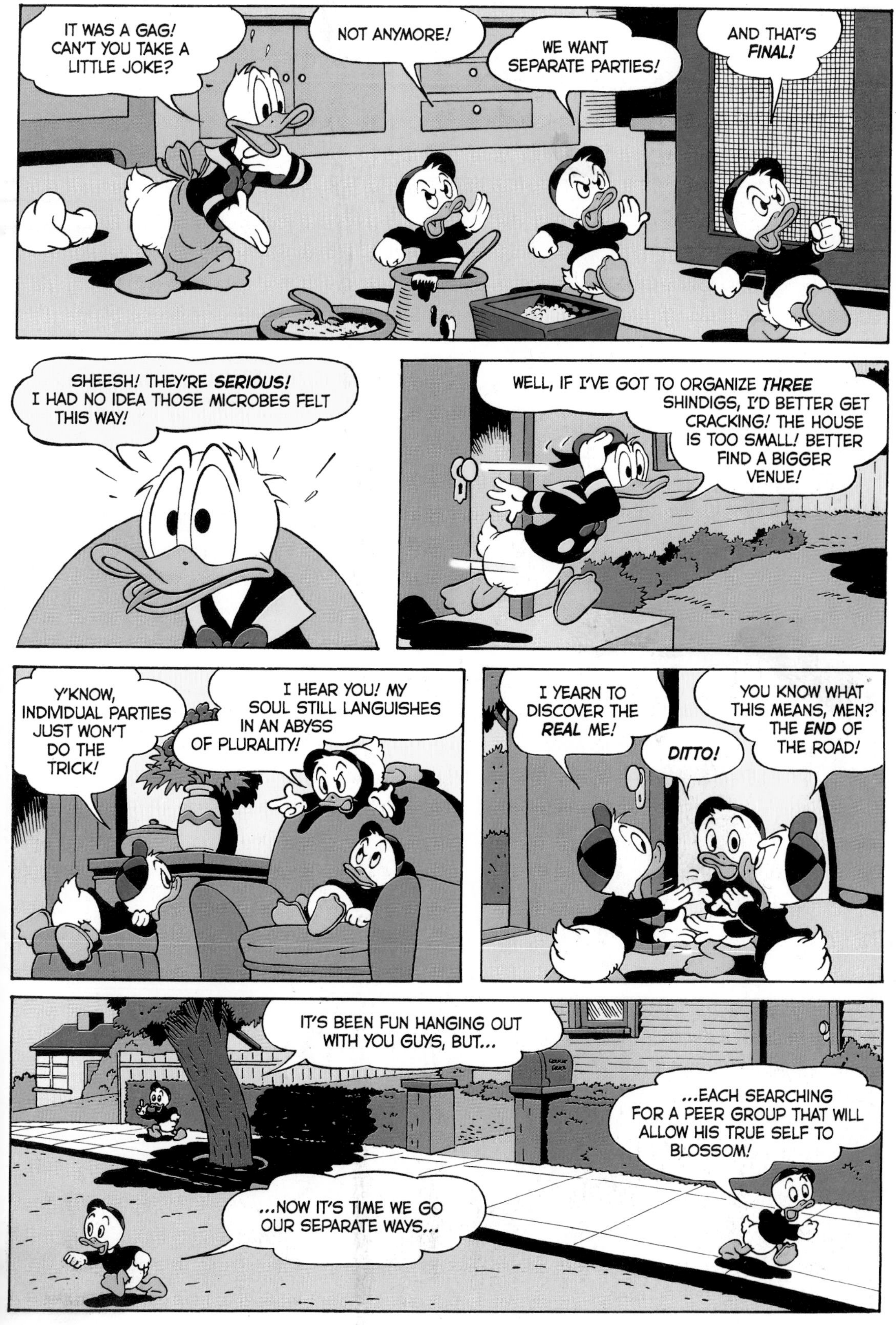
IT WAS A GAG! CAN'T YOU TAKE A LITTLE JOKE?
NOT ANYMORE!
WE WANT SEPARATE PARTIES!
AND THAT'S *FINAL!*
SHEESH! THEY'RE *SERIOUS!* I HAD NO IDEA THOSE MICROBES FELT THIS WAY!
WELL, IF I'VE GOT TO ORGANIZE *THREE* SHINDIGS, I'D BETTER GET CRACKING! THE HOUSE IS TOO SMALL! BETTER FIND A BIGGER VENUE!
Y'KNOW, INDIVIDUAL PARTIES JUST WON'T DO THE TRICK!
I HEAR YOU! MY SOUL STILL LANGUISHES IN AN ABYSS OF PLURALITY!
I YEARN TO DISCOVER THE *REAL* ME!
DITTO!
YOU KNOW WHAT THIS MEANS, MEN? THE *END* OF THE ROAD!
IT'S BEEN FUN HANGING OUT WITH YOU GUYS, BUT...
...NOW IT'S TIME WE GO OUR SEPARATE WAYS...
...EACH SEARCHING FOR A PEER GROUP THAT WILL ALLOW HIS TRUE SELF TO BLOSSOM!

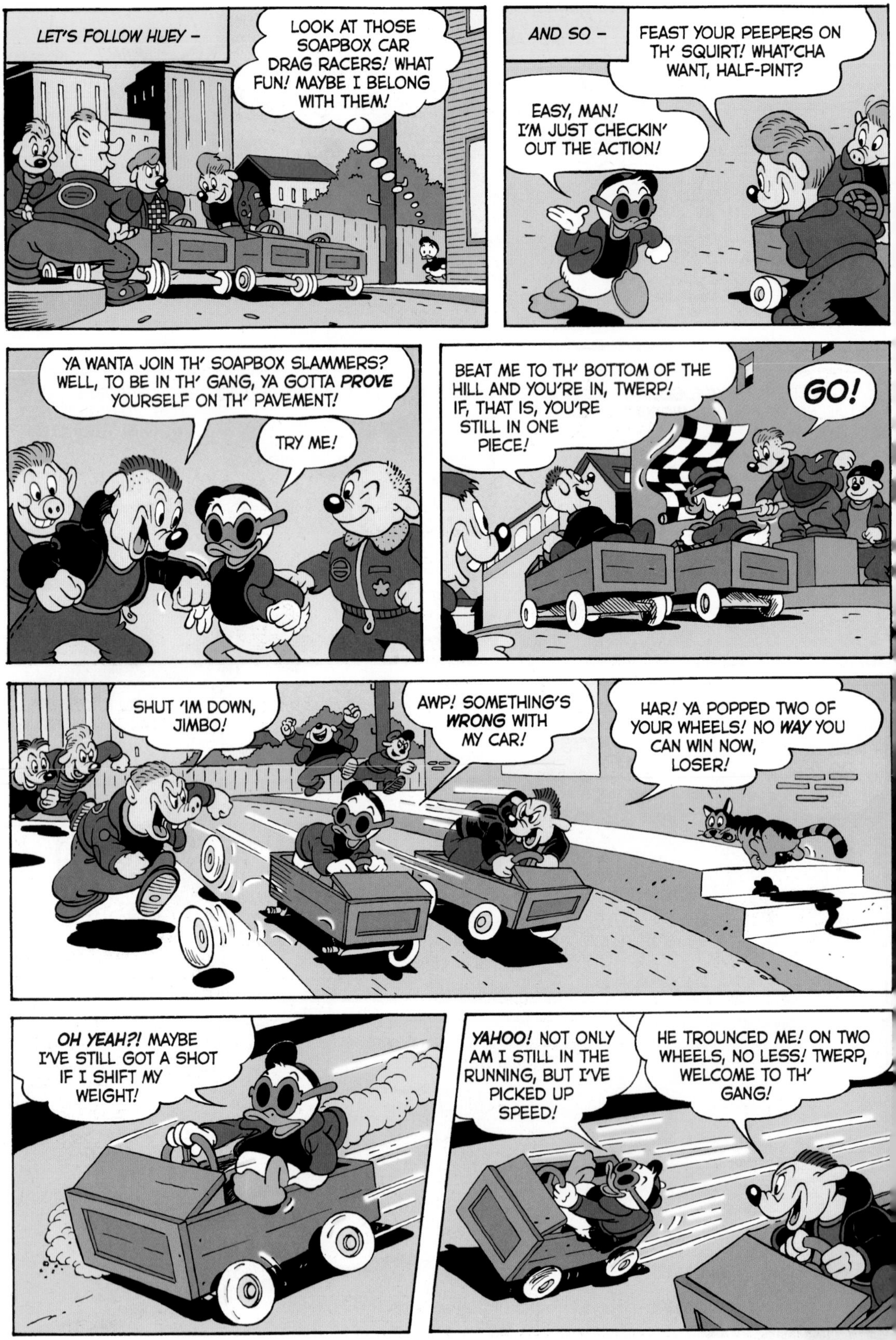
LET'S FOLLOW HUEY –
LOOK AT THOSE SOAPBOX CAR DRAG RACERS! WHAT FUN! MAYBE I BELONG WITH THEM!
AND SO –
FEAST YOUR PEEPERS ON TH' SQUIRT! WHAT'CHA WANT, HALF-PINT?
EASY, MAN! I'M JUST CHECKIN' OUT THE ACTION!
YA WANTA JOIN TH' SOAPBOX SLAMMERS? WELL, TO BE IN TH' GANG, YA GOTTA PROVE YOURSELF ON TH' PAVEMENT!
TRY ME!
BEAT ME TO TH' BOTTOM OF THE HILL AND YOU'RE IN, TWERP! IF, THAT IS, YOU'RE STILL IN ONE PIECE!
GO!
SHUT 'IM DOWN, JIMBO!
AWP! SOMETHING'S WRONG WITH MY CAR!
HAR! YA POPPED TWO OF YOUR WHEELS! NO WAY YOU CAN WIN NOW, LOSER!
OH YEAH?! MAYBE I'VE STILL GOT A SHOT IF I SHIFT MY WEIGHT!
YAHOO! NOT ONLY AM I STILL IN THE RUNNING, BUT I'VE PICKED UP SPEED!
HE TROUNCED ME! ON TWO WHEELS, NO LESS! TWERP, WELCOME TO TH' GANG!

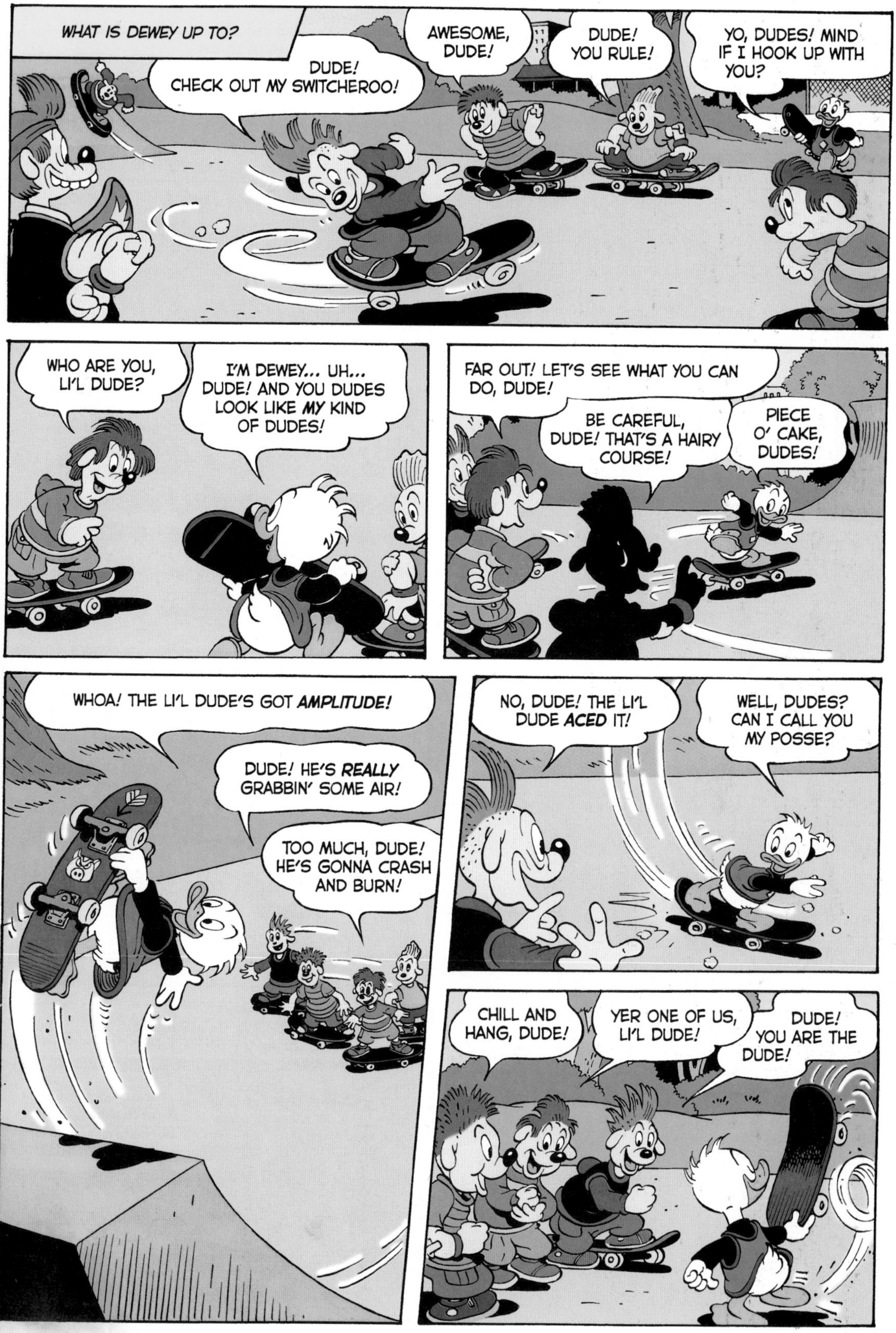
WHAT IS DEWEY UP TO?
DUDE! CHECK OUT MY SWITCHEROO!
AWESOME, DUDE!
DUDE! YOU RULE!
YO, DUDES! MIND IF I HOOK UP WITH YOU?
WHO ARE YOU, LI'L DUDE?
I'M DEWEY... UH... DUDE! AND YOU DUDES LOOK LIKE MY KIND OF DUDES!
FAR OUT! LET'S SEE WHAT YOU CAN DO, DUDE!
BE CAREFUL, DUDE! THAT'S A HAIRY COURSE!
PIECE O' CAKE, DUDES!
WHOA! THE LI'L DUDE'S GOT AMPLITUDE!
DUDE! HE'S REALLY GRABBIN' SOME AIR!
TOO MUCH, DUDE! HE'S GONNA CRASH AND BURN!
NO, DUDE! THE LI'L DUDE ACED IT!
WELL, DUDES? CAN I CALL YOU MY POSSE?
CHILL AND HANG, DUDE!
YER ONE OF US, LI'L DUDE!
DUDE! YOU ARE THE DUDE!

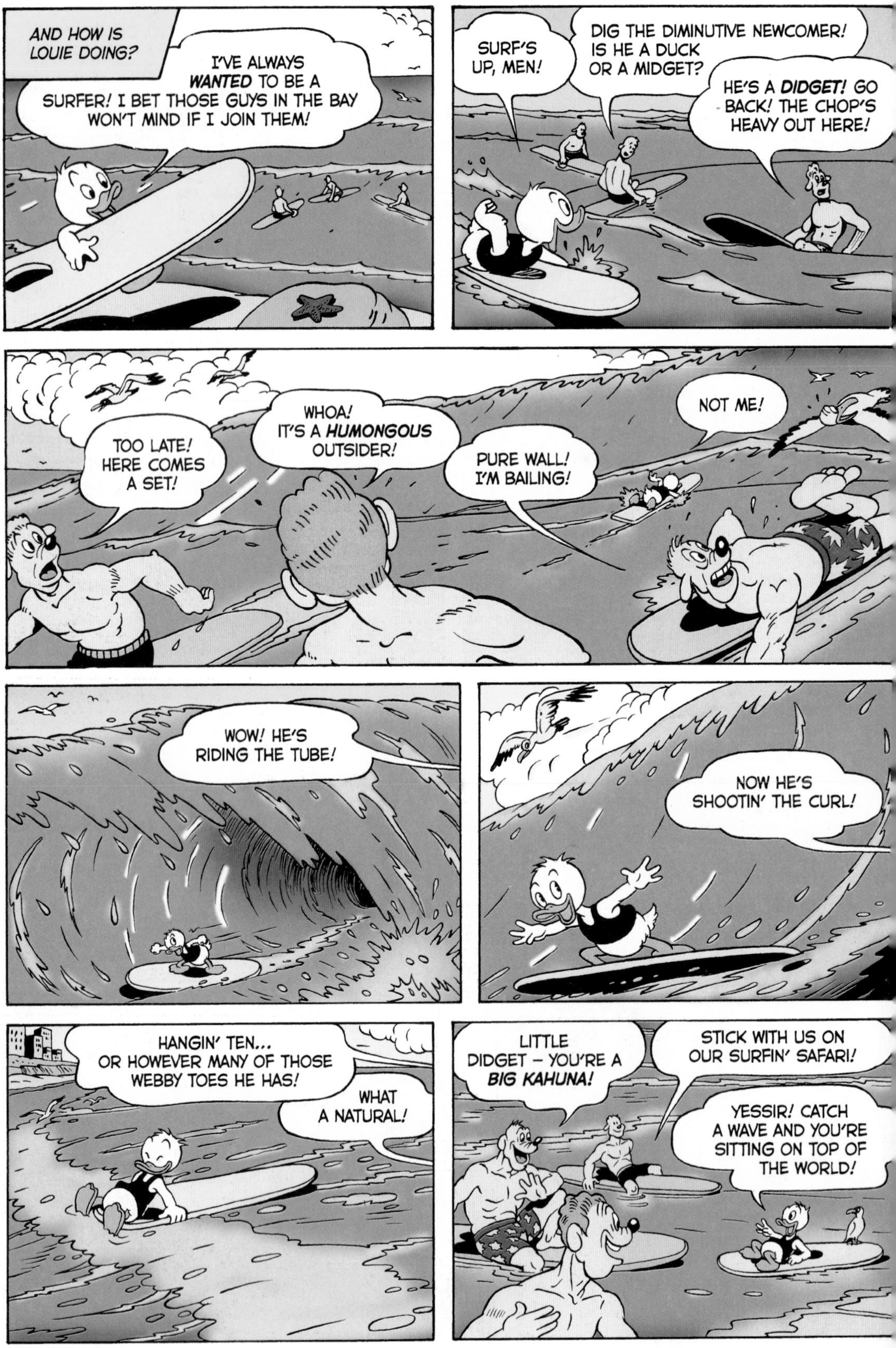
AND HOW IS LOUIE DOING?
I'VE ALWAYS WANTED TO BE A SURFER! I BET THOSE GUYS IN THE BAY WON'T MIND IF I JOIN THEM!
SURF'S UP, MEN!
DIG THE DIMINUTIVE NEWCOMER! IS HE A DUCK OR A MIDGET?
HE'S A DIDGET! GO BACK! THE CHOP'S HEAVY OUT HERE!
TOO LATE! HERE COMES A SET!
WHOA! IT'S A HUMONGOUS OUTSIDER!
PURE WALL! I'M BAILING!
NOT ME!
WOW! HE'S RIDING THE TUBE!
NOW HE'S SHOOTIN' THE CURL!
HANGIN' TEN... OR HOWEVER MANY OF THOSE WEBBY TOES HE HAS!
WHAT A NATURAL!
LITTLE DIDGET – YOU'RE A BIG KAHUNA!
STICK WITH US ON OUR SURFIN' SAFARI!
YESSIR! CATCH A WAVE AND YOU'RE SITTING ON TOP OF THE WORLD!

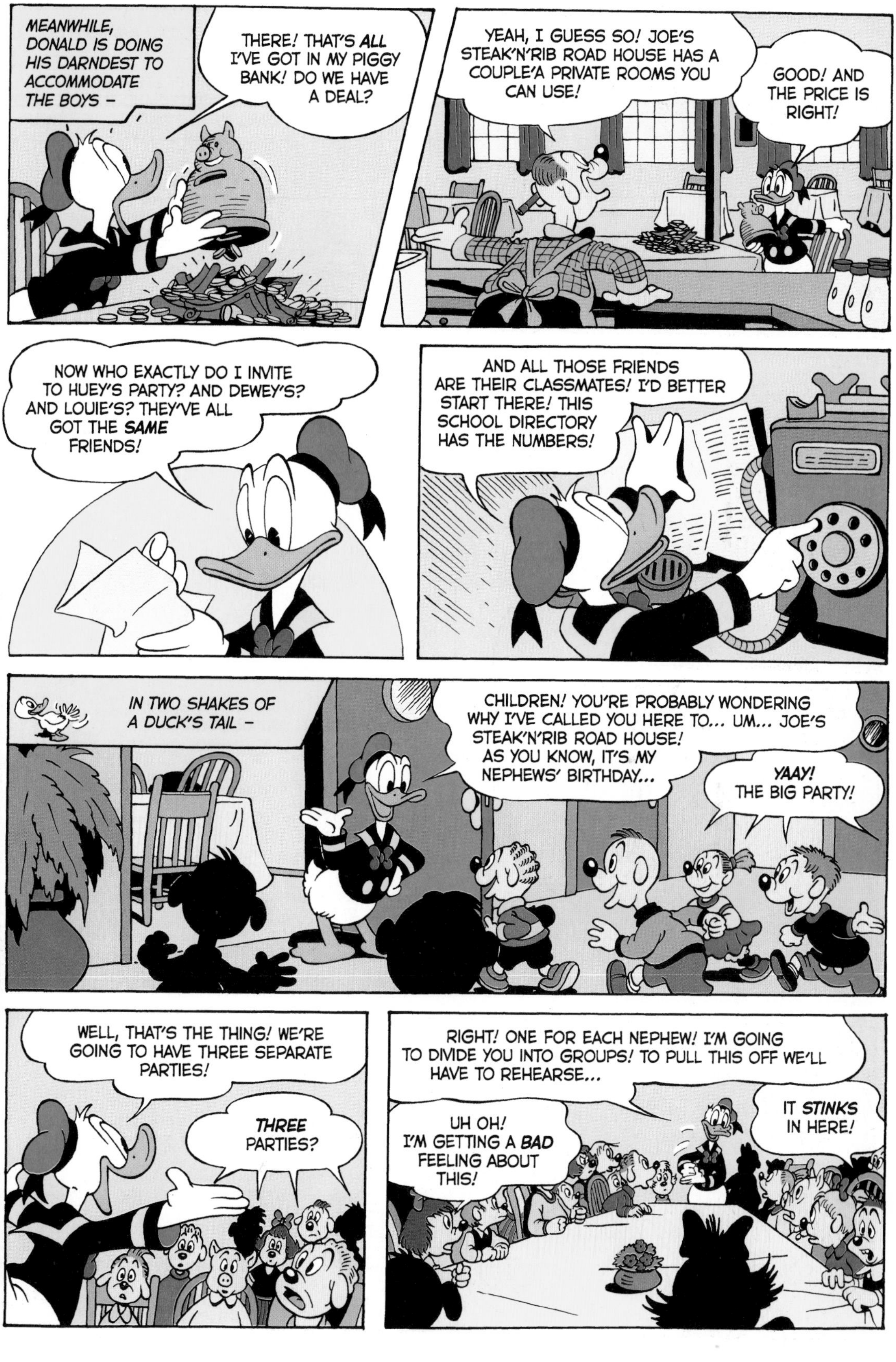

MEANWHILE, DONALD IS DOING HIS DARNDEST TO ACCOMMODATE THE BOYS –
THERE! THAT'S ALL I'VE GOT IN MY PIGGY BANK! DO WE HAVE A DEAL?
YEAH, I GUESS SO! JOE'S STEAK'N'RIB ROAD HOUSE HAS A COUPLE'A PRIVATE ROOMS YOU CAN USE!
GOOD! AND THE PRICE IS RIGHT!
NOW WHO EXACTLY DO I INVITE TO HUEY'S PARTY? AND DEWEY'S? AND LOUIE'S? THEY'VE ALL GOT THE SAME FRIENDS!
AND ALL THOSE FRIENDS ARE THEIR CLASSMATES! I'D BETTER START THERE! THIS SCHOOL DIRECTORY HAS THE NUMBERS!
IN TWO SHAKES OF A DUCK'S TAIL –
CHILDREN! YOU'RE PROBABLY WONDERING WHY I'VE CALLED YOU HERE TO... UM... JOE'S STEAK'N'RIB ROAD HOUSE! AS YOU KNOW, IT'S MY NEPHEWS' BIRTHDAY...
YAAY! THE BIG PARTY!
WELL, THAT'S THE THING! WE'RE GOING TO HAVE THREE SEPARATE PARTIES!
THREE PARTIES?
RIGHT! ONE FOR EACH NEPHEW! I'M GOING TO DIVIDE YOU INTO GROUPS! TO PULL THIS OFF WE'LL HAVE TO REHEARSE...
UH OH! I'M GETTING A BAD FEELING ABOUT THIS!
IT STINKS IN HERE!

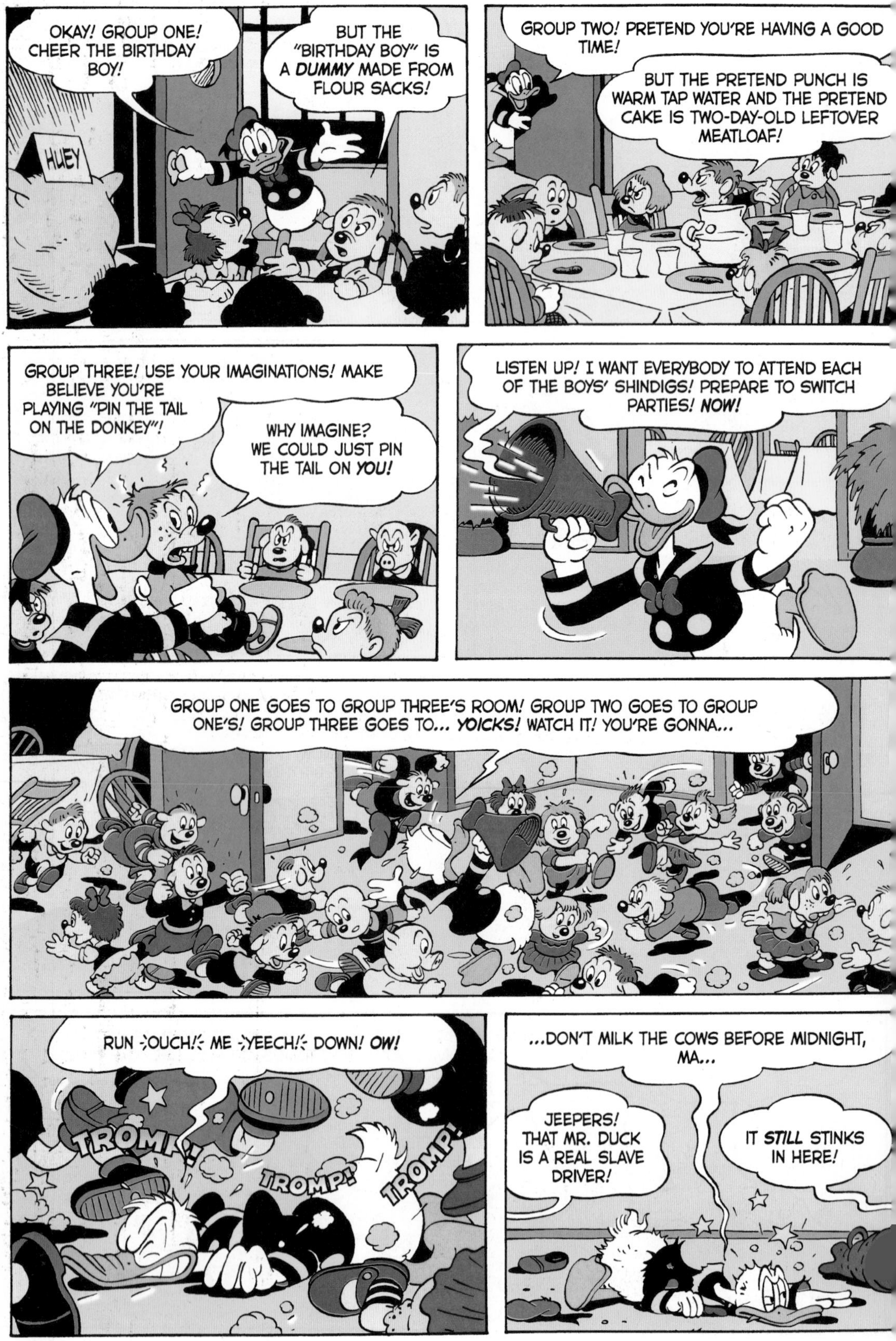
OKAY! GROUP ONE! CHEER THE BIRTHDAY BOY!
BUT THE "BIRTHDAY BOY" IS A DUMMY MADE FROM FLOUR SACKS!
HUEY
GROUP TWO! PRETEND YOU'RE HAVING A GOOD TIME!
BUT THE PRETEND PUNCH IS WARM TAP WATER AND THE PRETEND CAKE IS TWO-DAY-OLD LEFTOVER MEATLOAF!
GROUP THREE! USE YOUR IMAGINATIONS! MAKE BELIEVE YOU'RE PLAYING "PIN THE TAIL ON THE DONKEY"!
WHY IMAGINE? WE COULD JUST PIN THE TAIL ON YOU!
LISTEN UP! I WANT EVERYBODY TO ATTEND EACH OF THE BOYS' SHINDIGS! PREPARE TO SWITCH PARTIES! NOW!
GROUP ONE GOES TO GROUP THREE'S ROOM! GROUP TWO GOES TO GROUP ONE'S! GROUP THREE GOES TO... YOICKS! WATCH IT! YOU'RE GONNA...
RUN -OUCH!- ME -YEECH!- DOWN! OW!
TROMP!
TROMP!
TROMP!
...DON'T MILK THE COWS BEFORE MIDNIGHT, MA...
JEEPERS! THAT MR. DUCK IS A REAL SLAVE DRIVER!
IT STILL STINKS IN HERE!

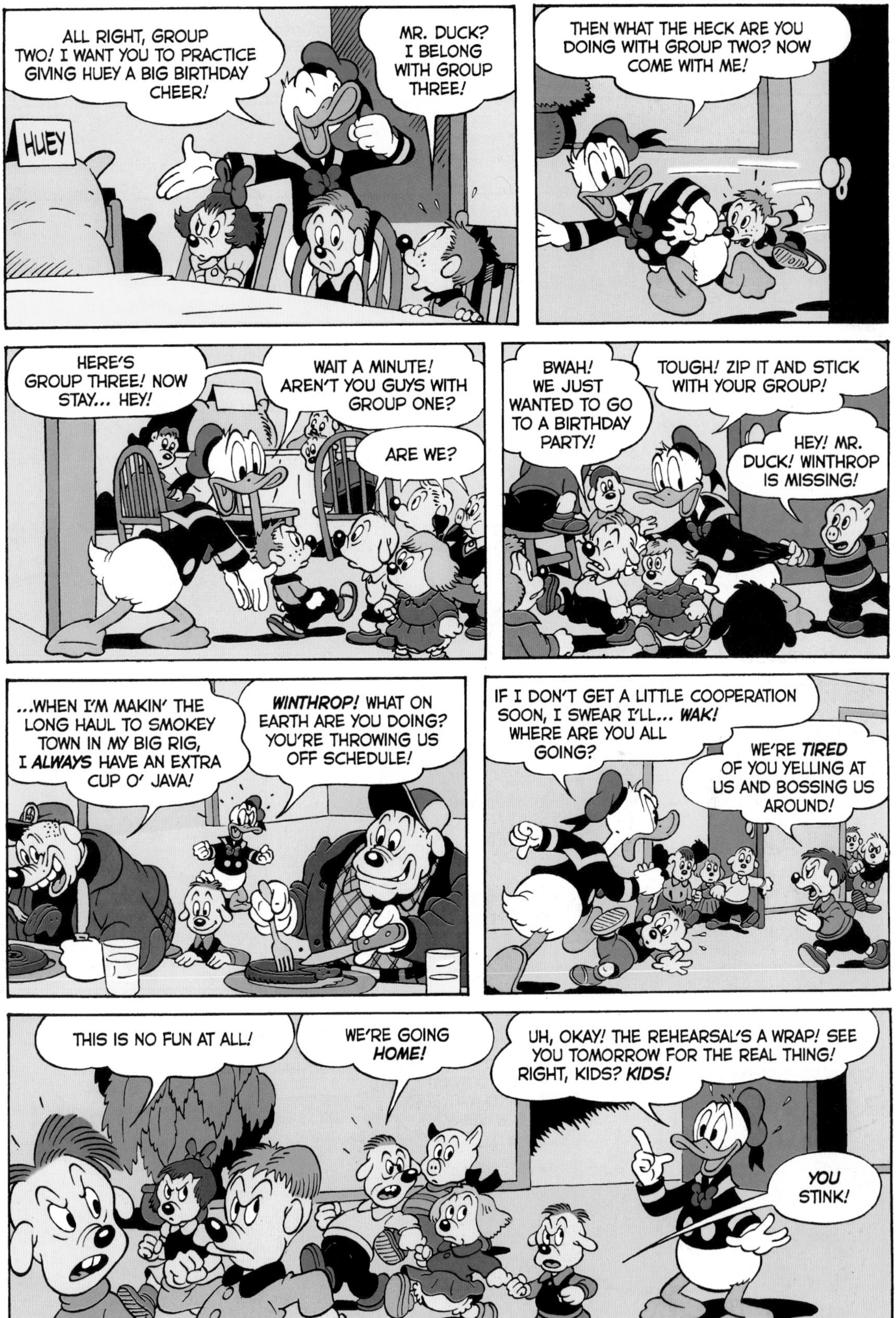
ALL RIGHT, GROUP TWO! I WANT YOU TO PRACTICE GIVING HUEY A BIG BIRTHDAY CHEER!
HUEY
MR. DUCK? I BELONG WITH GROUP THREE!
THEN WHAT THE HECK ARE YOU DOING WITH GROUP TWO? NOW COME WITH ME!
HERE'S GROUP THREE! NOW STAY... HEY!
WAIT A MINUTE! AREN'T YOU GUYS WITH GROUP ONE?
ARE WE?
BWAH! WE JUST WANTED TO GO TO A BIRTHDAY PARTY!
TOUGH! ZIP IT AND STICK WITH YOUR GROUP!
HEY! MR. DUCK! WINTHROP IS MISSING!
...WHEN I'M MAKIN' THE LONG HAUL TO SMOKEY TOWN IN MY BIG RIG, I *ALWAYS* HAVE AN EXTRA CUP O' JAVA!
WINTHROP! WHAT ON EARTH ARE YOU DOING? YOU'RE THROWING US OFF SCHEDULE!
IF I DON'T GET A LITTLE COOPERATION SOON, I SWEAR I'LL... *WAK!* WHERE ARE YOU ALL GOING?
WE'RE *TIRED* OF YOU YELLING AT US AND BOSSING US AROUND!
THIS IS NO FUN AT ALL!
WE'RE GOING *HOME!*
UH, OKAY! THE REHEARSAL'S A WRAP! SEE YOU TOMORROW FOR THE REAL THING! RIGHT, KIDS? *KIDS!*
YOU STINK!

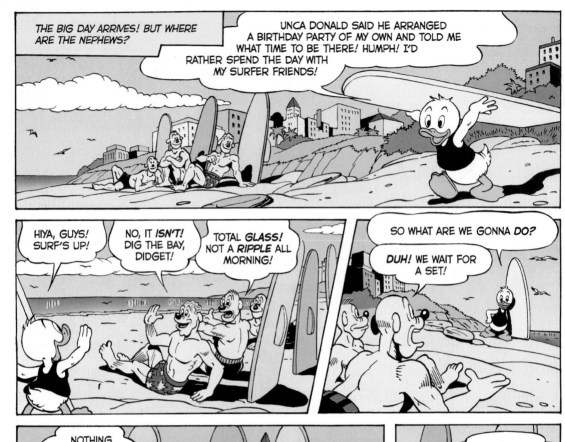

THE BIG DAY ARRIVES! BUT WHERE ARE THE NEPHEWS?

UNCA DONALD SAID HE ARRANGED A BIRTHDAY PARTY OF MY OWN AND TOLD ME WHAT TIME TO BE THERE! HUMPH! I'D RATHER SPEND THE DAY WITH MY SURFER FRIENDS!

HIYA, GUYS! SURF'S UP!

NO, IT *ISN'T!* DIG THE BAY, DIDGET!

TOTAL *GLASS!* NOT A *RIPPLE* ALL MORNING!

SO WHAT ARE WE GONNA *DO?*

DUH! WE WAIT FOR A *SET!*

NOTHING ELSE WE *CAN* DO!

I KNOW! LET'S PLAY A *GAME!*

LET'S BE LEGIONNAIRES IN THE SAHARA! OR COWBOYS CROSSING THE GREAT MOJAVE!

WHAT ARE YOU *TALKING* ABOUT?

SIT DOWN, DIDGET, AND WAIT FOR THE WAVES!

WOW! THESE GUYS ARE ABSOLUTELY *BANKRUPT* IN THE IMAGINATION DEPARTMENT! THAT PARTY'S STARTING TO SOUND PRETTY GOOD...

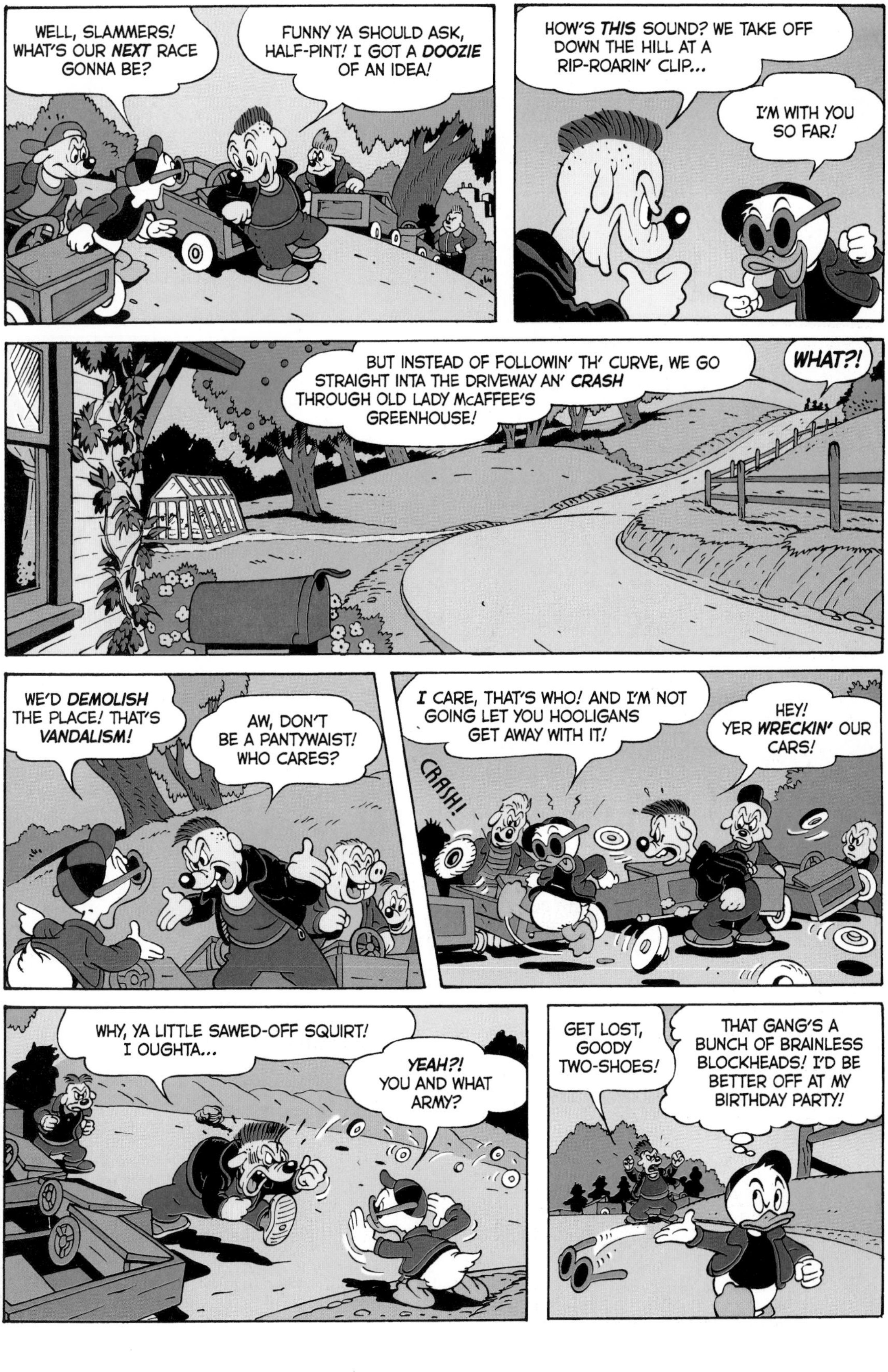
WELL, SLAMMERS! WHAT'S OUR NEXT RACE GONNA BE?
FUNNY YA SHOULD ASK, HALF-PINT! I GOT A DOOZIE OF AN IDEA!
HOW'S THIS SOUND? WE TAKE OFF DOWN THE HILL AT A RIP-ROARIN' CLIP...
I'M WITH YOU SO FAR!
BUT INSTEAD OF FOLLOWIN' TH' CURVE, WE GO STRAIGHT INTA THE DRIVEWAY AN' CRASH THROUGH OLD LADY McAFFEE'S GREENHOUSE!
WHAT?!
WE'D DEMOLISH THE PLACE! THAT'S VANDALISM!
AW, DON'T BE A PANTYWAIST! WHO CARES?
I CARE, THAT'S WHO! AND I'M NOT GOING LET YOU HOOLIGANS GET AWAY WITH IT!
HEY! YER WRECKIN' OUR CARS!
CRASH!
WHY, YA LITTLE SAWED-OFF SQUIRT! I OUGHTA...
YEAH?! YOU AND WHAT ARMY?
GET LOST, GOODY TWO-SHOES!
THAT GANG'S A BUNCH OF BRAINLESS BLOCKHEADS! I'D BE BETTER OFF AT MY BIRTHDAY PARTY!

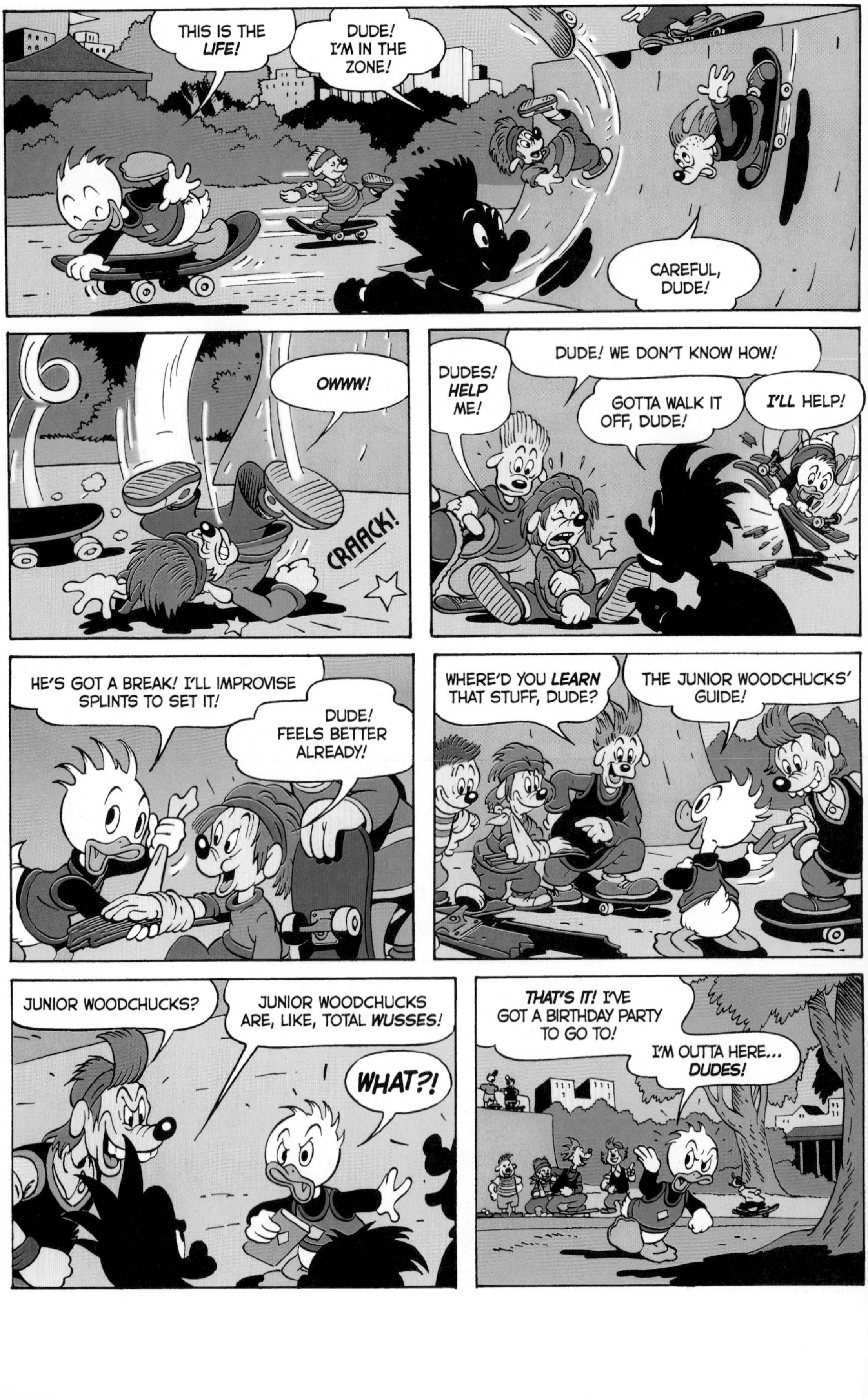
THIS IS THE *LIFE!*
DUDE! I'M IN THE ZONE!
CAREFUL, DUDE!
OWWW!
CRAACK!
DUDES! *HELP* ME!
DUDE! WE DON'T KNOW HOW!
GOTTA WALK IT OFF, DUDE!
I'LL HELP!
HE'S GOT A BREAK! I'LL IMPROVISE SPLINTS TO SET IT!
DUDE! FEELS BETTER ALREADY!
WHERE'D YOU *LEARN* THAT STUFF, DUDE?
THE JUNIOR WOODCHUCKS' GUIDE!
JUNIOR WOODCHUCKS?
JUNIOR WOODCHUCKS ARE, LIKE, TOTAL *WUSSES!*
WHAT?!
THAT'S IT! I'VE GOT A BIRTHDAY PARTY TO GO TO!
I'M OUTTA HERE... *DUDES!*

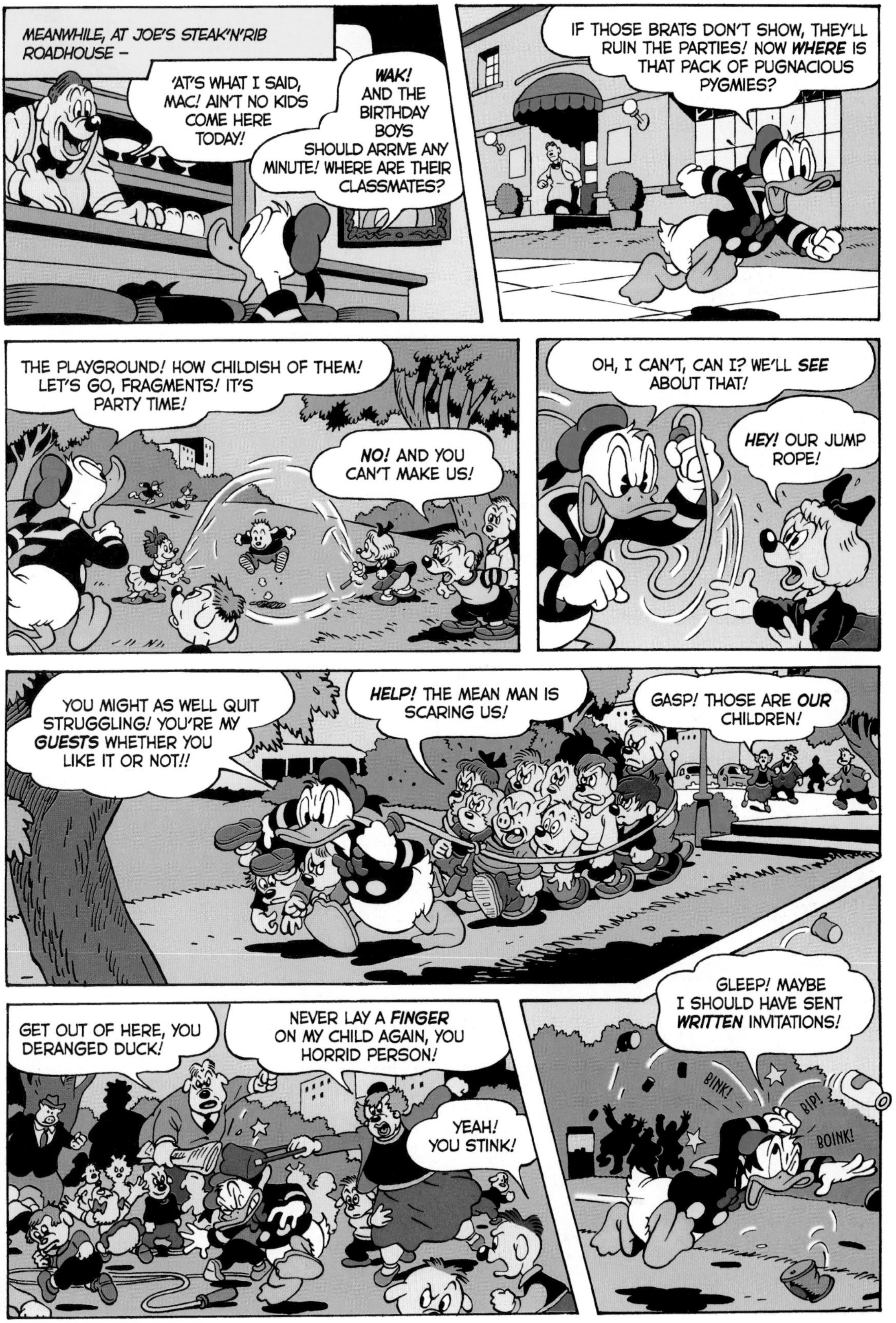

MEANWHILE, AT JOE'S STEAK'N'RIB ROADHOUSE –
'AT'S WHAT I SAID, MAC! AIN'T NO KIDS COME HERE TODAY!
WAK! AND THE BIRTHDAY BOYS SHOULD ARRIVE ANY MINUTE! WHERE ARE THEIR CLASSMATES?
IF THOSE BRATS DON'T SHOW, THEY'LL RUIN THE PARTIES! NOW WHERE IS THAT PACK OF PUGNACIOUS PYGMIES?
THE PLAYGROUND! HOW CHILDISH OF THEM! LET'S GO, FRAGMENTS! IT'S PARTY TIME!
NO! AND YOU CAN'T MAKE US!
OH, I CAN'T, CAN I? WE'LL SEE ABOUT THAT!
HEY! OUR JUMP ROPE!
YOU MIGHT AS WELL QUIT STRUGGLING! YOU'RE MY GUESTS WHETHER YOU LIKE IT OR NOT!!
HELP! THE MEAN MAN IS SCARING US!
GASP! THOSE ARE OUR CHILDREN!
GET OUT OF HERE, YOU DERANGED DUCK!
NEVER LAY A FINGER ON MY CHILD AGAIN, YOU HORRID PERSON!
YEAH! YOU STINK!
GLEEP! MAYBE I SHOULD HAVE SENT WRITTEN INVITATIONS!
BINK!
BIP!
BOINK!

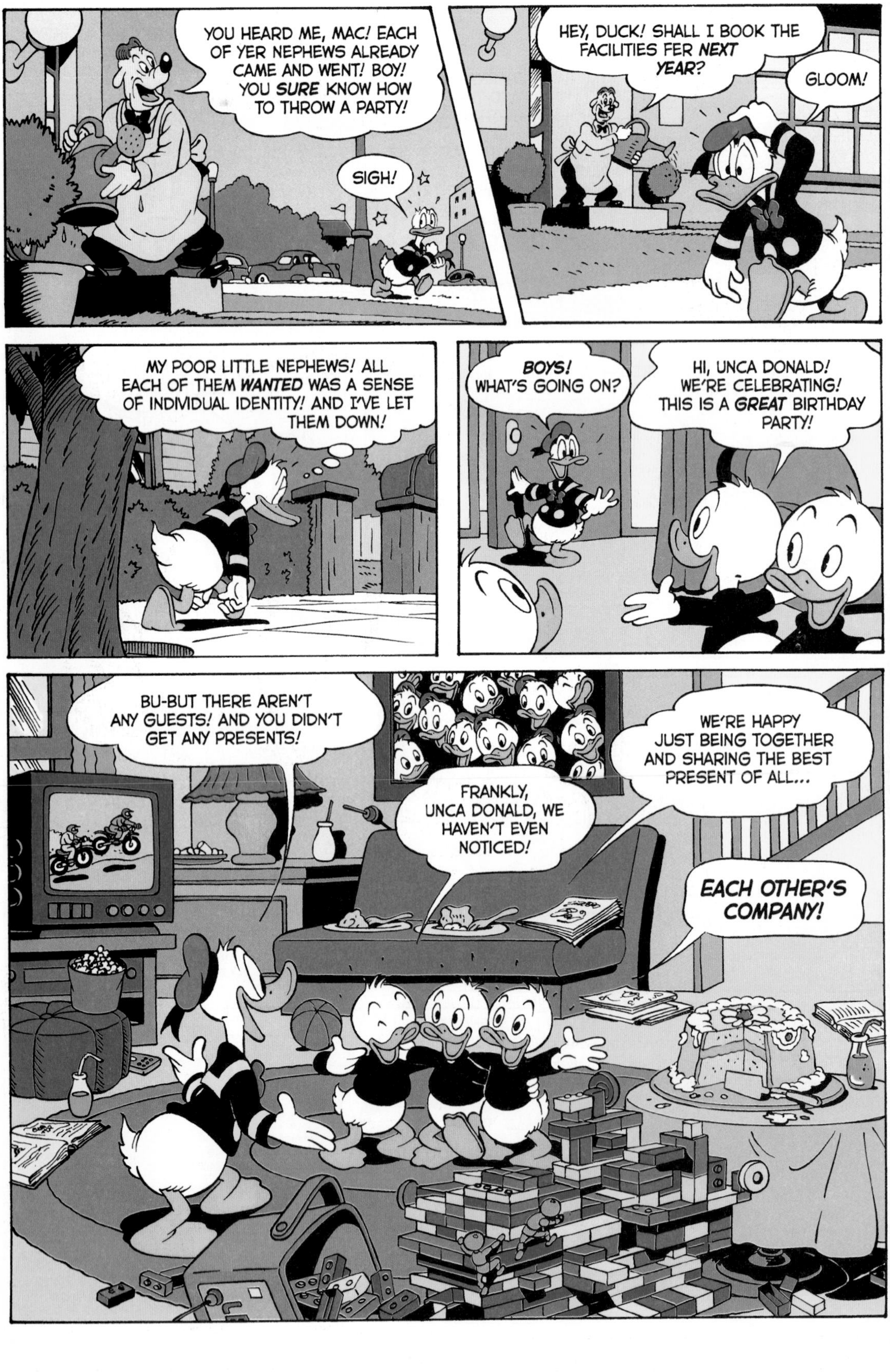
YOU HEARD ME, MAC! EACH OF YER NEPHEWS ALREADY CAME AND WENT! BOY! YOU SURE KNOW HOW TO THROW A PARTY!
SIGH!
HEY, DUCK! SHALL I BOOK THE FACILITIES FER NEXT YEAR?
GLOOM!
MY POOR LITTLE NEPHEWS! ALL EACH OF THEM WANTED WAS A SENSE OF INDIVIDUAL IDENTITY! AND I'VE LET THEM DOWN!
BOYS! WHAT'S GOING ON?
HI, UNCA DONALD! WE'RE CELEBRATING! THIS IS A GREAT BIRTHDAY PARTY!
BU-BUT THERE AREN'T ANY GUESTS! AND YOU DIDN'T GET ANY PRESENTS!
FRANKLY, UNCA DONALD, WE HAVEN'T EVEN NOTICED!
WE'RE HAPPY JUST BEING TOGETHER AND SHARING THE BEST PRESENT OF ALL...
EACH OTHER'S COMPANY!

Uncle Scrooge is in another bind. Can Donald and the boys save him from the Peeweegahs? ("What's a Peeweegah," you ask?)

UH OH!

©2007 Disney Enterprises, Inc.

Learn all about Peeweegahs and Wendigos in *Walt Disney's Uncle Scrooge Adventures—The Barks/Rosa Collection*. This new series features stories by famed writers/illustrators Carl Barks and Don Rosa. Each volume contains an original Carl Barks classic followed by a Don Rosa sequel. Volume One kicks things off with "Land of the Pygmy Indians" and "War of the Wendigo."

GEMSTONE
PUBLISHING

Disney comics are available at your local comic shop and online at
www.gemstonepub.com/disney.

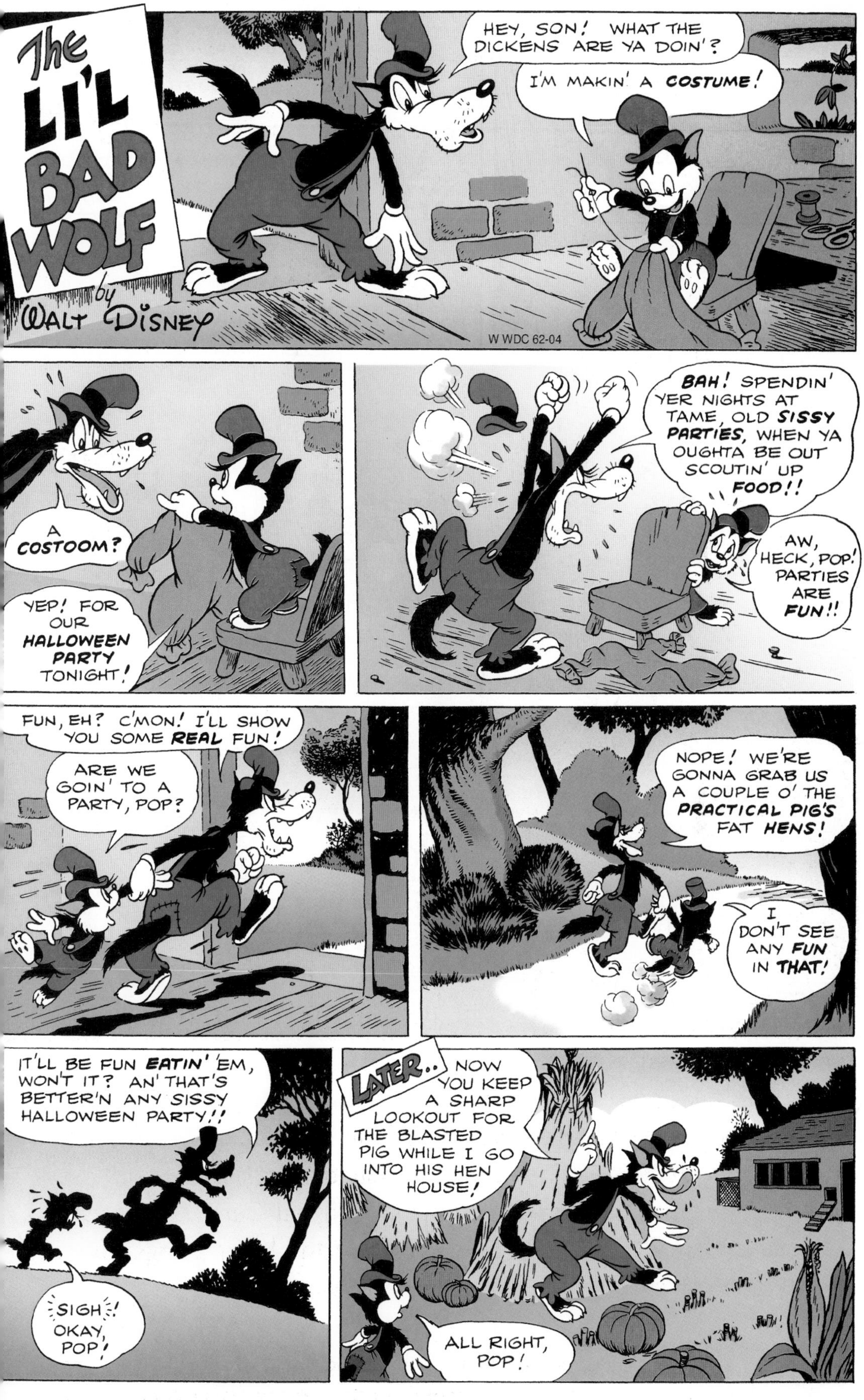
The LI'L BAD WOLF
by WALT DISNEY
HEY, SON! WHAT THE DICKENS ARE YA DOIN'?
I'M MAKIN' A COSTUME!
W WDC 62-04
A COSTOOM?
YEP! FOR OUR HALLOWEEN PARTY TONIGHT!
BAH! SPENDIN' YER NIGHTS AT TAME, OLD SISSY PARTIES, WHEN YA OUGHTA BE OUT SCOUTIN' UP FOOD!!
AW, HECK, POP! PARTIES ARE FUN!!
FUN, EH? C'MON! I'LL SHOW YOU SOME REAL FUN!
ARE WE GOIN' TO A PARTY, POP?
NOPE! WE'RE GONNA GRAB US A COUPLE O' THE PRACTICAL PIG'S FAT HENS!
I DON'T SEE ANY FUN IN THAT!
IT'LL BE FUN EATIN' 'EM, WON'T IT? AN' THAT'S BETTER'N ANY SISSY HALLOWEEN PARTY!!
SIGH! OKAY, POP!
LATER..
NOW YOU KEEP A SHARP LOOKOUT FOR THE BLASTED PIG WHILE I GO INTO HIS HEN HOUSE!
ALL RIGHT, POP!

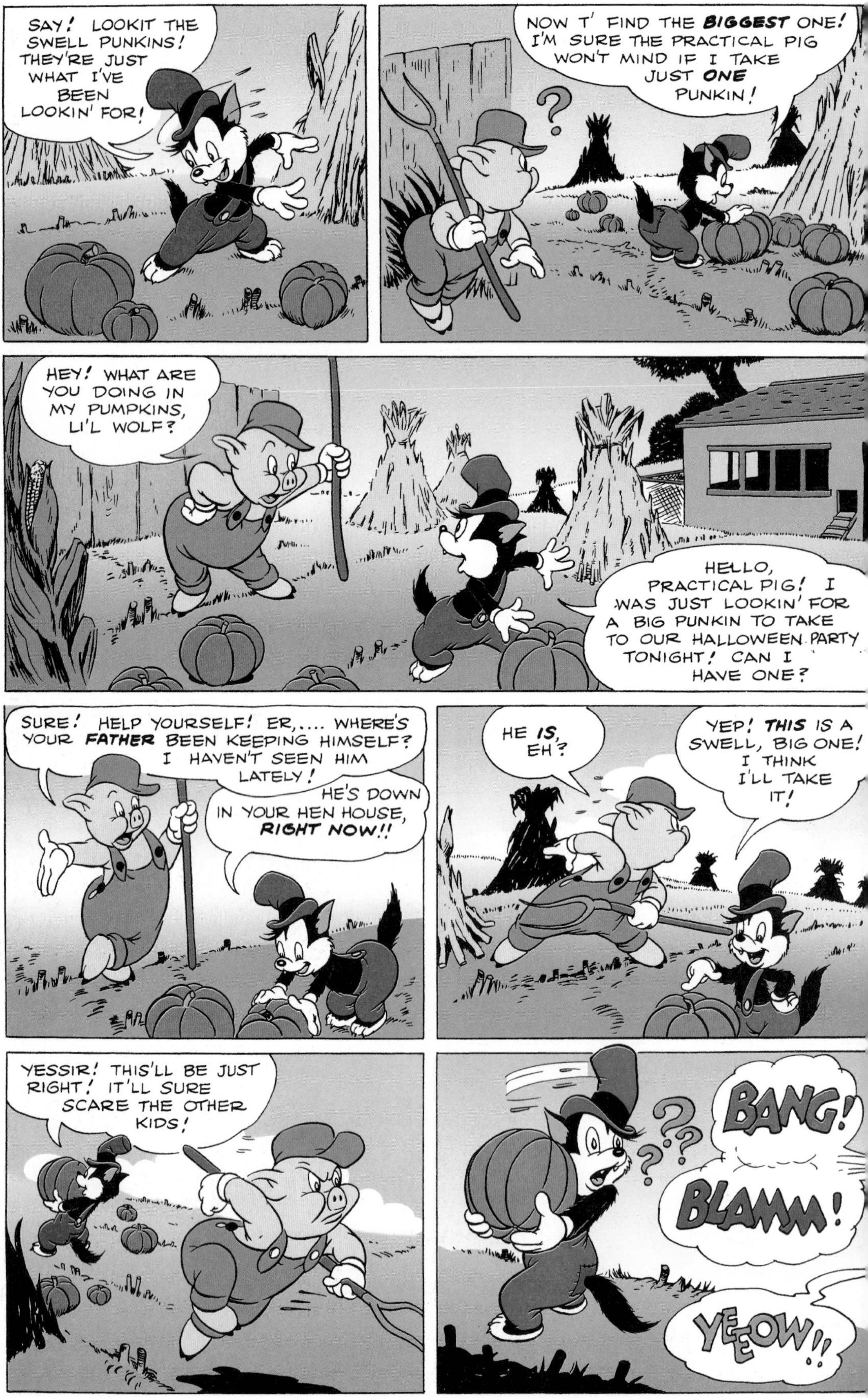
SAY! LOOKIT THE SWELL PUNKINS! THEY'RE JUST WHAT I'VE BEEN LOOKIN' FOR!
NOW T' FIND THE BIGGEST ONE! I'M SURE THE PRACTICAL PIG WON'T MIND IF I TAKE JUST ONE PUNKIN!
?
HEY! WHAT ARE YOU DOING IN MY PUMPKINS, LI'L WOLF?
HELLO, PRACTICAL PIG! I WAS JUST LOOKIN' FOR A BIG PUNKIN TO TAKE TO OUR HALLOWEEN PARTY TONIGHT! CAN I HAVE ONE?
SURE! HELP YOURSELF! ER,.... WHERE'S YOUR FATHER BEEN KEEPING HIMSELF? I HAVEN'T SEEN HIM LATELY!
HE'S DOWN IN YOUR HEN HOUSE, RIGHT NOW!!
HE IS, EH?
YEP! THIS IS A SWELL, BIG ONE! I THINK I'LL TAKE IT!
YESSIR! THIS'LL BE JUST RIGHT! IT'LL SURE SCARE THE OTHER KIDS!
???
BANG!
BLAMM!
YEEOW!!

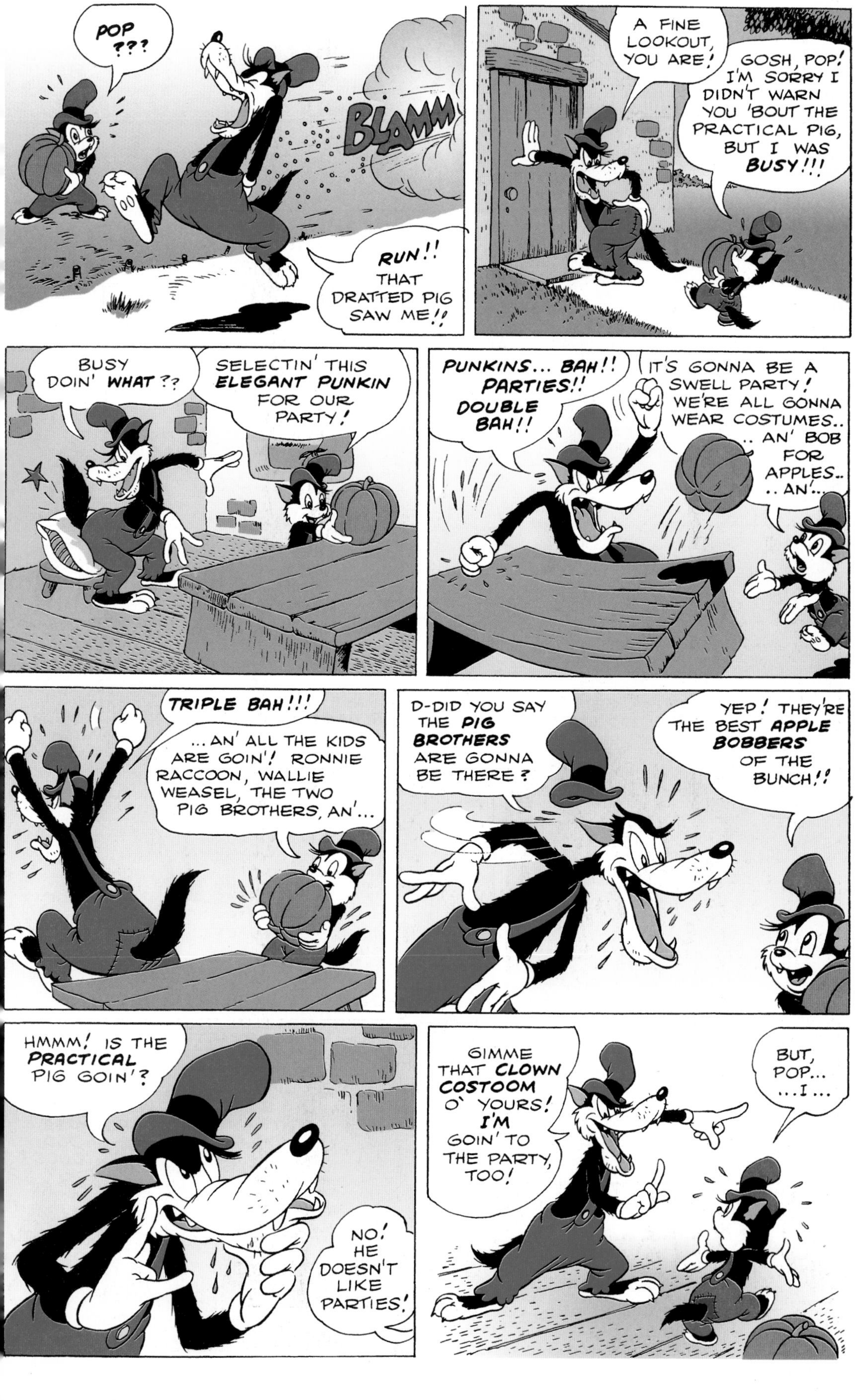
POP ???
BLAMM
RUN!! THAT DRATTED PIG SAW ME!!
A FINE LOOKOUT, YOU ARE!
GOSH, POP! I'M SORRY I DIDN'T WARN YOU 'BOUT THE PRACTICAL PIG, BUT I WAS BUSY!!!
BUSY DOIN' WHAT??
SELECTIN' THIS ELEGANT PUNKIN FOR OUR PARTY!
PUNKINS... BAH!! PARTIES!! DOUBLE BAH!!
IT'S GONNA BE A SWELL PARTY! WE'RE ALL GONNA WEAR COSTUMES.. .. AN' BOB FOR APPLES.. .. AN'...
TRIPLE BAH!!!
...AN' ALL THE KIDS ARE GOIN'! RONNIE RACCOON, WALLIE WEASEL, THE TWO PIG BROTHERS, AN'...
D-DID YOU SAY THE PIG BROTHERS ARE GONNA BE THERE?
YEP! THEY'RE THE BEST APPLE BOBBERS OF THE BUNCH!!
HMMM! IS THE PRACTICAL PIG GOIN'?
NO! HE DOESN'T LIKE PARTIES!
GIMME THAT CLOWN COSTOOM O' YOURS! I'M GOIN' TO THE PARTY, TOO!
BUT, POP... ...I...

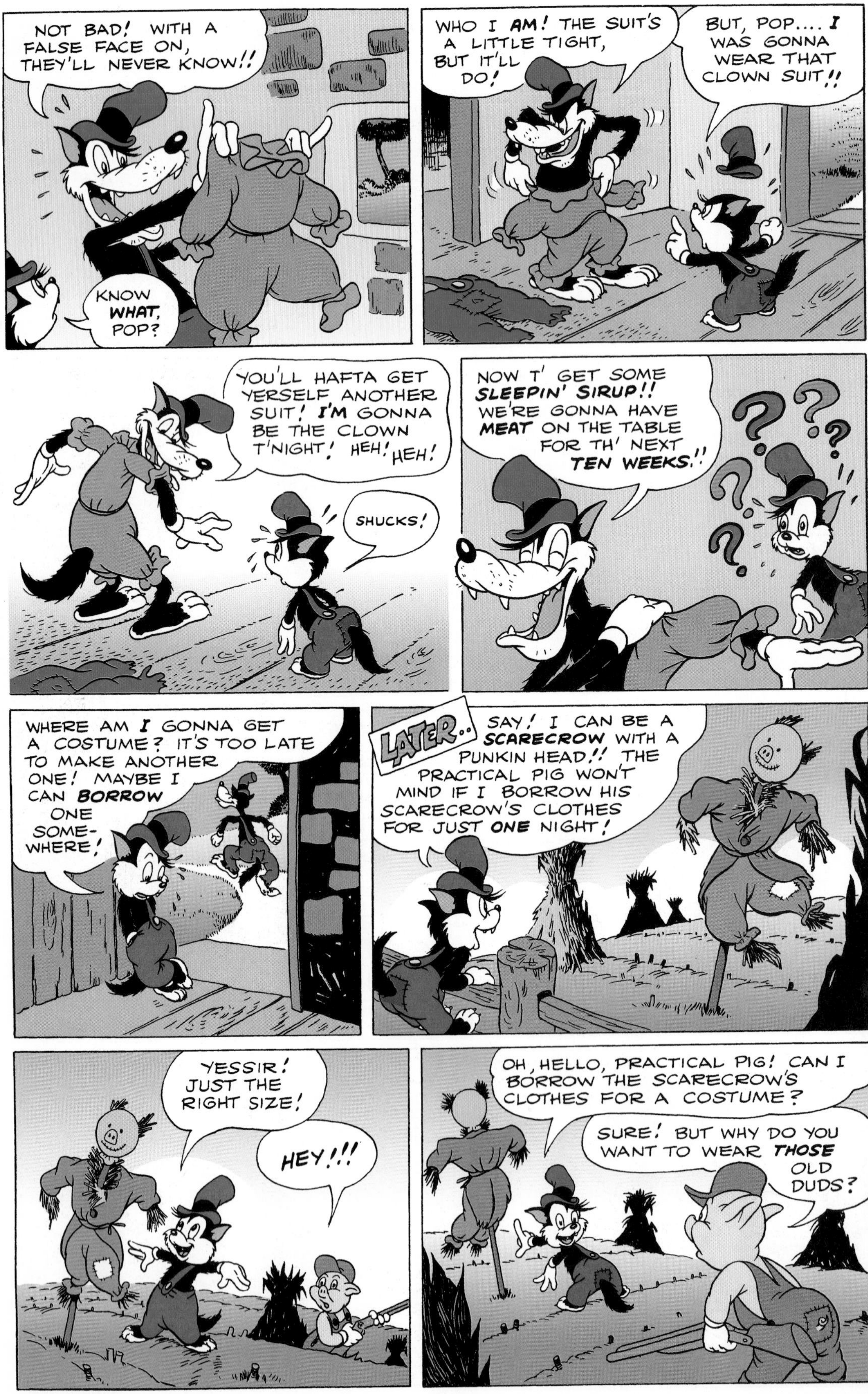

NOT BAD! WITH A FALSE FACE ON, THEY'LL NEVER KNOW!!
KNOW WHAT, POP?
WHO I AM! THE SUIT'S A LITTLE TIGHT, BUT IT'LL DO!
BUT, POP.... I WAS GONNA WEAR THAT CLOWN SUIT!!
YOU'LL HAFTA GET YERSELF ANOTHER SUIT! I'M GONNA BE THE CLOWN T'NIGHT! HEH! HEH!
SHUCKS!
NOW T' GET SOME SLEEPIN' SIRUP!! WE'RE GONNA HAVE MEAT ON THE TABLE FOR TH' NEXT TEN WEEKS!!
WHERE AM I GONNA GET A COSTUME? IT'S TOO LATE TO MAKE ANOTHER ONE! MAYBE I CAN BORROW ONE SOMEWHERE!
LATER..
SAY! I CAN BE A SCARECROW WITH A PUNKIN HEAD!! THE PRACTICAL PIG WON'T MIND IF I BORROW HIS SCARECROW'S CLOTHES FOR JUST ONE NIGHT!
YESSIR! JUST THE RIGHT SIZE!
HEY!!!
OH, HELLO, PRACTICAL PIG! CAN I BORROW THE SCARECROW'S CLOTHES FOR A COSTUME?
SURE! BUT WHY DO YOU WANT TO WEAR THOSE OLD DUDS?

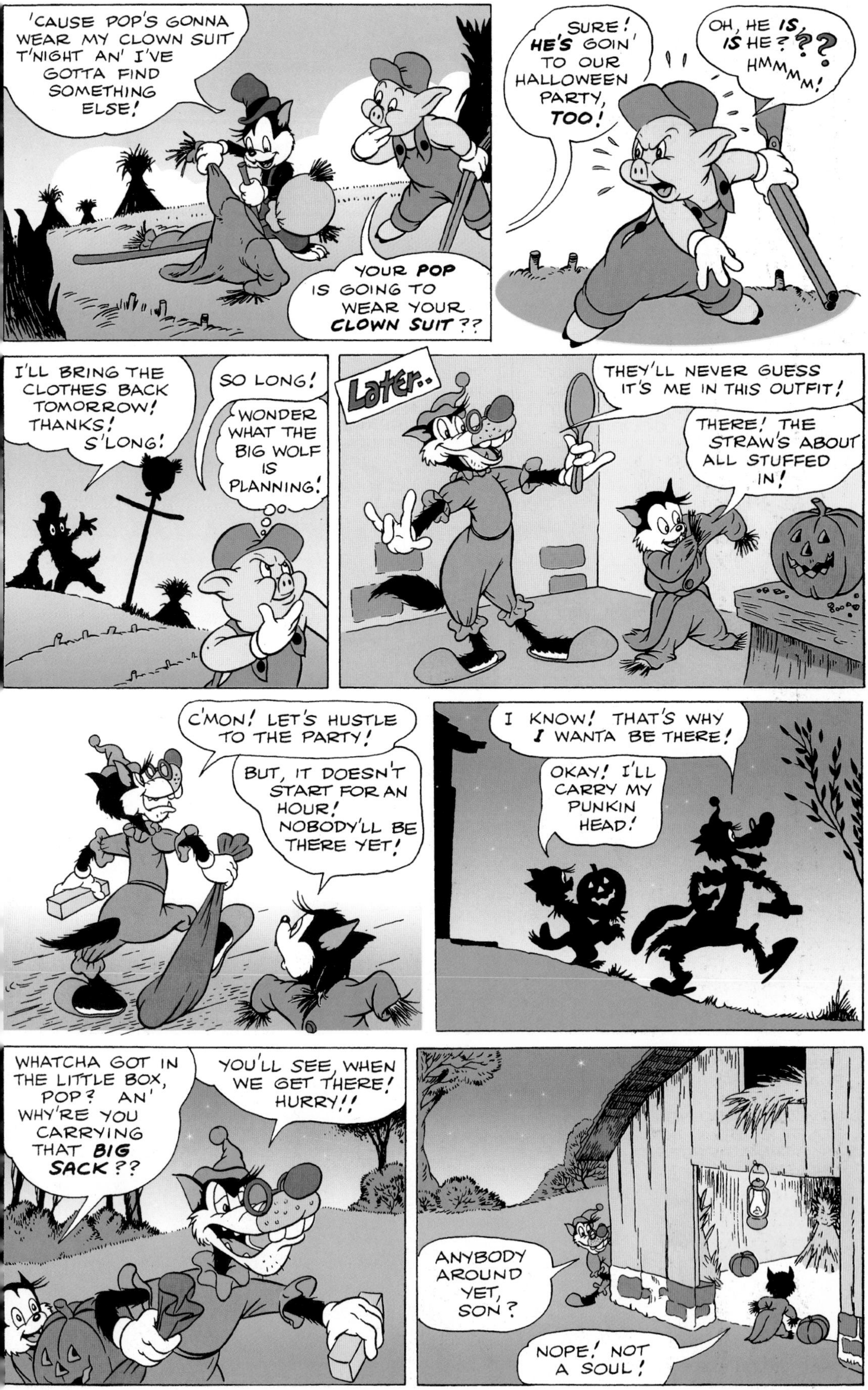
'CAUSE POP'S GONNA WEAR MY CLOWN SUIT T'NIGHT AN' I'VE GOTTA FIND SOMETHING ELSE!
YOUR POP IS GOING TO WEAR YOUR CLOWN SUIT??
SURE! HE'S GOIN' TO OUR HALLOWEEN PARTY, TOO!
OH, HE IS, IS HE??? HMMMM!
I'LL BRING THE CLOTHES BACK TOMORROW! THANKS! S'LONG!
SO LONG!
WONDER WHAT THE BIG WOLF IS PLANNING!
Later..
THEY'LL NEVER GUESS IT'S ME IN THIS OUTFIT!
THERE! THE STRAW'S ABOUT ALL STUFFED IN!
C'MON! LET'S HUSTLE TO THE PARTY!
BUT, IT DOESN'T START FOR AN HOUR! NOBODY'LL BE THERE YET!
I KNOW! THAT'S WHY I WANTA BE THERE!
OKAY! I'LL CARRY MY PUNKIN HEAD!
WHATCHA GOT IN THE LITTLE BOX, POP? AN' WHY'RE YOU CARRYING THAT BIG SACK??
YOU'LL SEE, WHEN WE GET THERE! HURRY!!
ANYBODY AROUND YET, SON?
NOPE! NOT A SOUL!

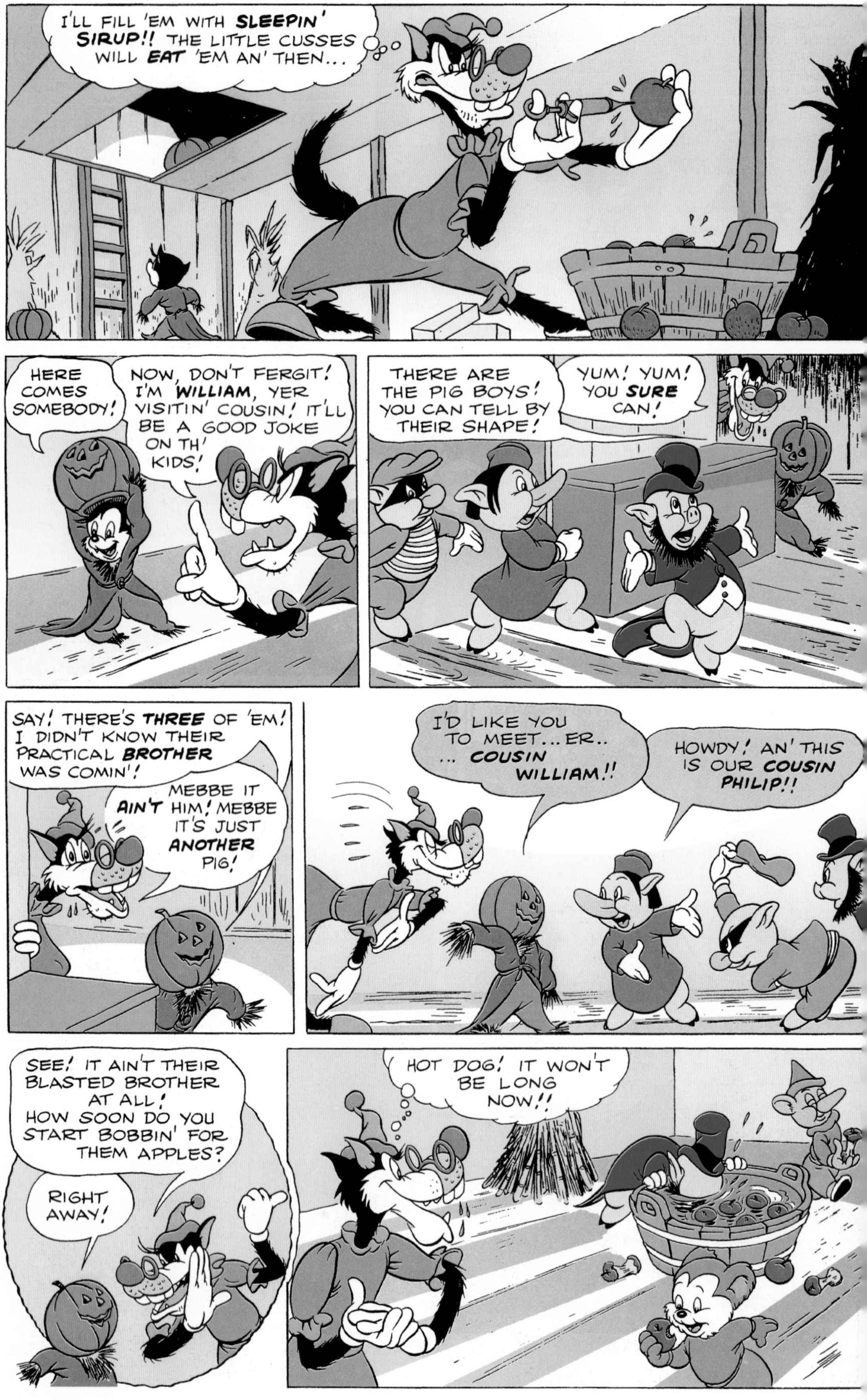
I'LL FILL 'EM WITH SLEEPIN' SIRUP!! THE LITTLE CUSSES WILL EAT 'EM AN' THEN...
HERE COMES SOMEBODY!
NOW, DON'T FERGIT! I'M WILLIAM, YER VISITIN' COUSIN! IT'LL BE A GOOD JOKE ON TH' KIDS!
THERE ARE THE PIG BOYS! YOU CAN TELL BY THEIR SHAPE!
YUM! YUM! YOU SURE CAN!
SAY! THERE'S THREE OF 'EM! I DIDN'T KNOW THEIR PRACTICAL BROTHER WAS COMIN'!
MEBBE IT AIN'T HIM! MEBBE IT'S JUST ANOTHER PIG!
I'D LIKE YOU TO MEET... ER.. ... COUSIN WILLIAM!!
HOWDY! AN' THIS IS OUR COUSIN PHILIP!!
SEE! IT AIN'T THEIR BLASTED BROTHER AT ALL! HOW SOON DO YOU START BOBBIN' FOR THEM APPLES?
RIGHT AWAY!
HOT DOG! IT WON'T BE LONG NOW!!

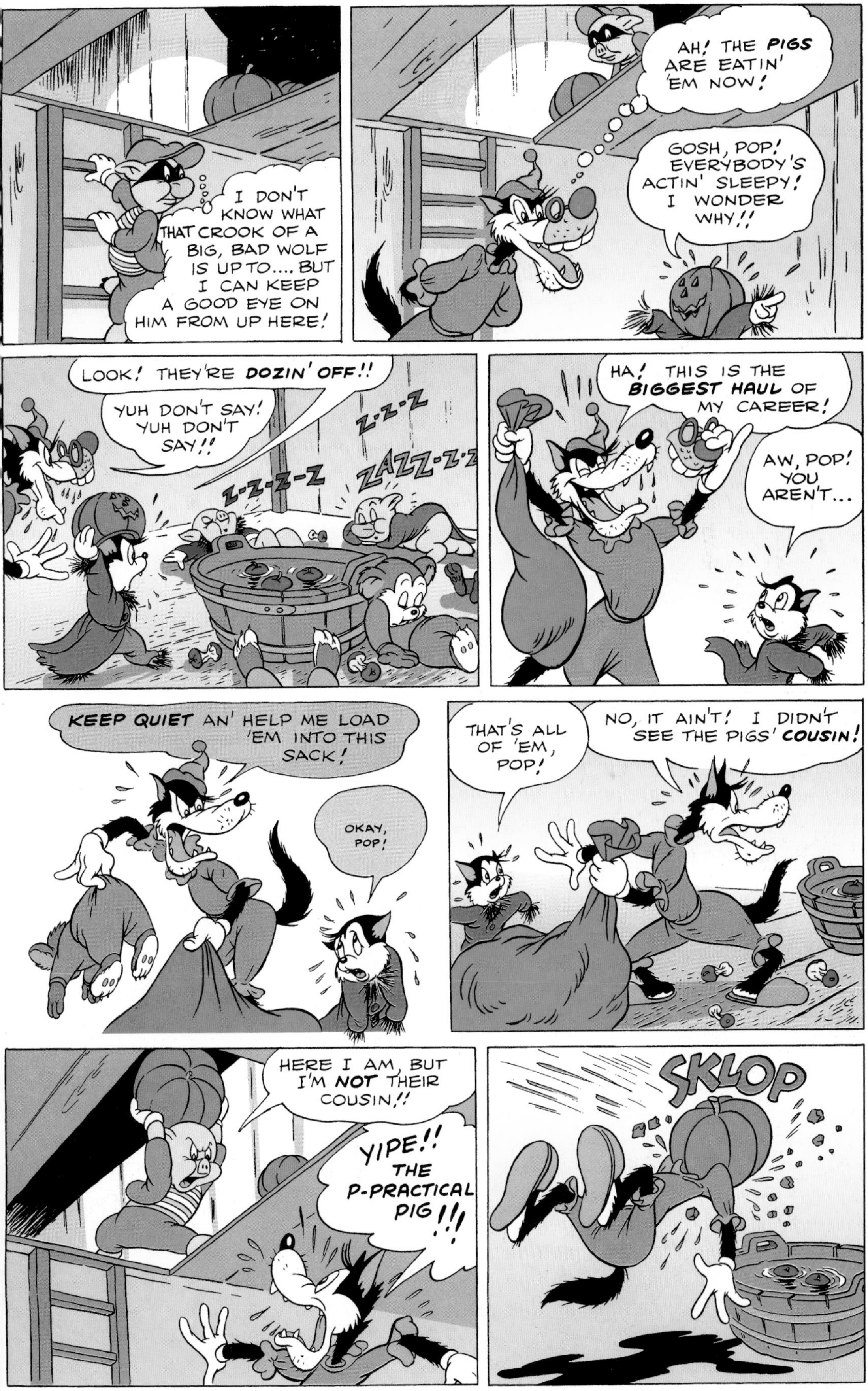
I DON'T KNOW WHAT THAT CROOK OF A BIG, BAD WOLF IS UP TO.... BUT I CAN KEEP A GOOD EYE ON HIM FROM UP HERE!
AH! THE PIGS ARE EATIN' 'EM NOW!
GOSH, POP! EVERYBODY'S ACTIN' SLEEPY! I WONDER WHY!!
LOOK! THEY'RE DOZIN' OFF!!
YUH DON'T SAY! YUH DON'T SAY!!
Z-Z-Z
Z-Z-Z-Z
ZAZZ-Z-Z
HA! THIS IS THE BIGGEST HAUL OF MY CAREER!
AW, POP! YOU AREN'T...
KEEP QUIET AN' HELP ME LOAD 'EM INTO THIS SACK!
OKAY, POP!
THAT'S ALL OF 'EM, POP!
NO, IT AIN'T! I DIDN'T SEE THE PIGS' COUSIN!
HERE I AM, BUT I'M NOT THEIR COUSIN!!
YIPE!! THE P-PRACTICAL PIG!!!
SKLOP

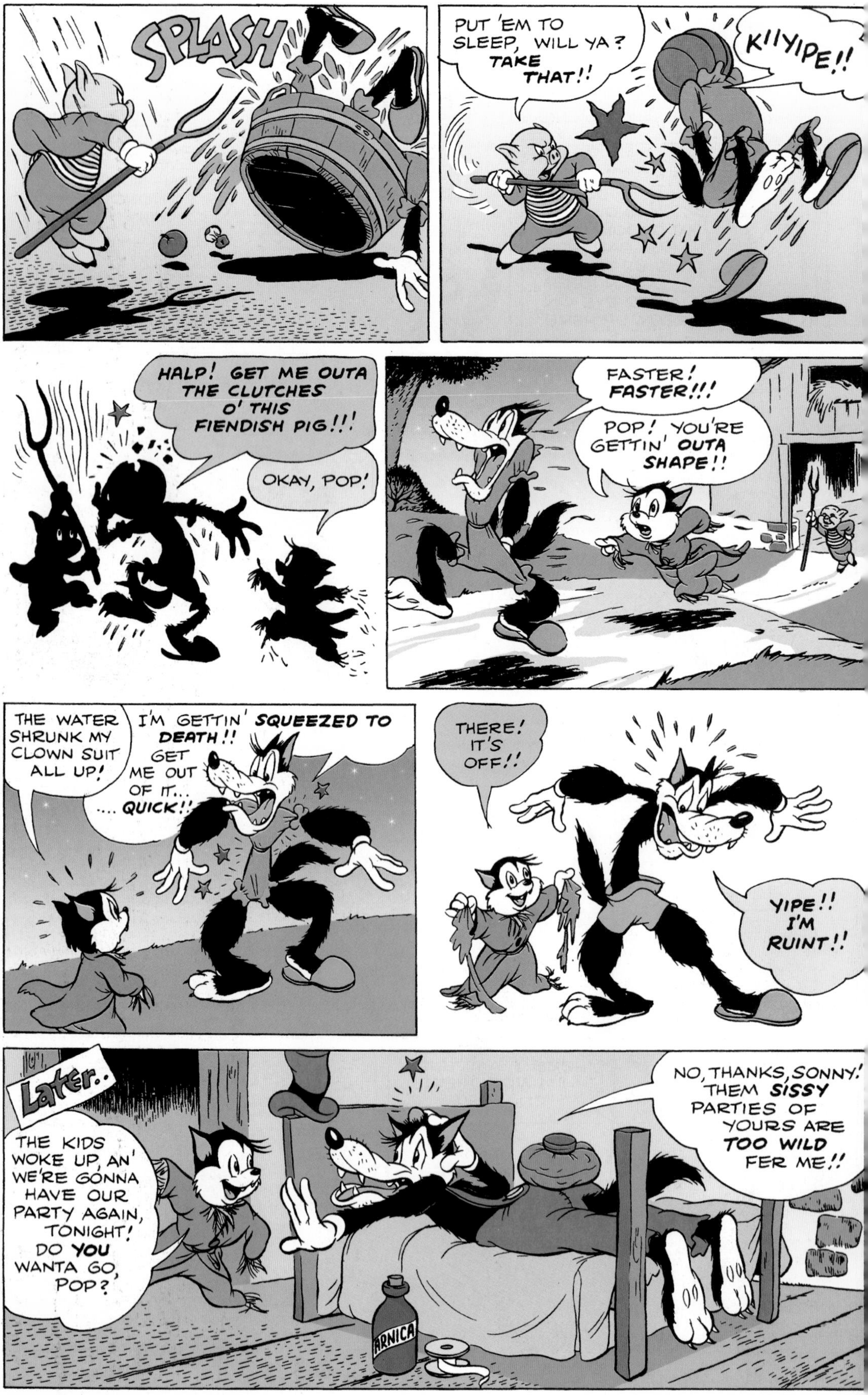
SPLASH
PUT 'EM TO SLEEP, WILL YA? TAKE THAT!!
KI'YIPE!!
HALP! GET ME OUTA THE CLUTCHES O' THIS FIENDISH PIG!!!
OKAY, POP!
FASTER! FASTER!!!
POP! YOU'RE GETTIN' OUTA SHAPE!!
THE WATER SHRUNK MY CLOWN SUIT ALL UP!
I'M GETTIN' SQUEEZED TO DEATH!! GET ME OUT OF IT.... QUICK!!
THERE! IT'S OFF!!
YIPE!! I'M RUINT!!
Later..
THE KIDS WOKE UP, AN' WE'RE GONNA HAVE OUR PARTY AGAIN, TONIGHT! DO YOU WANTA GO, POP?
NO, THANKS, SONNY! THEM SISSY PARTIES OF YOURS ARE TOO WILD FER ME!!
ARNICA

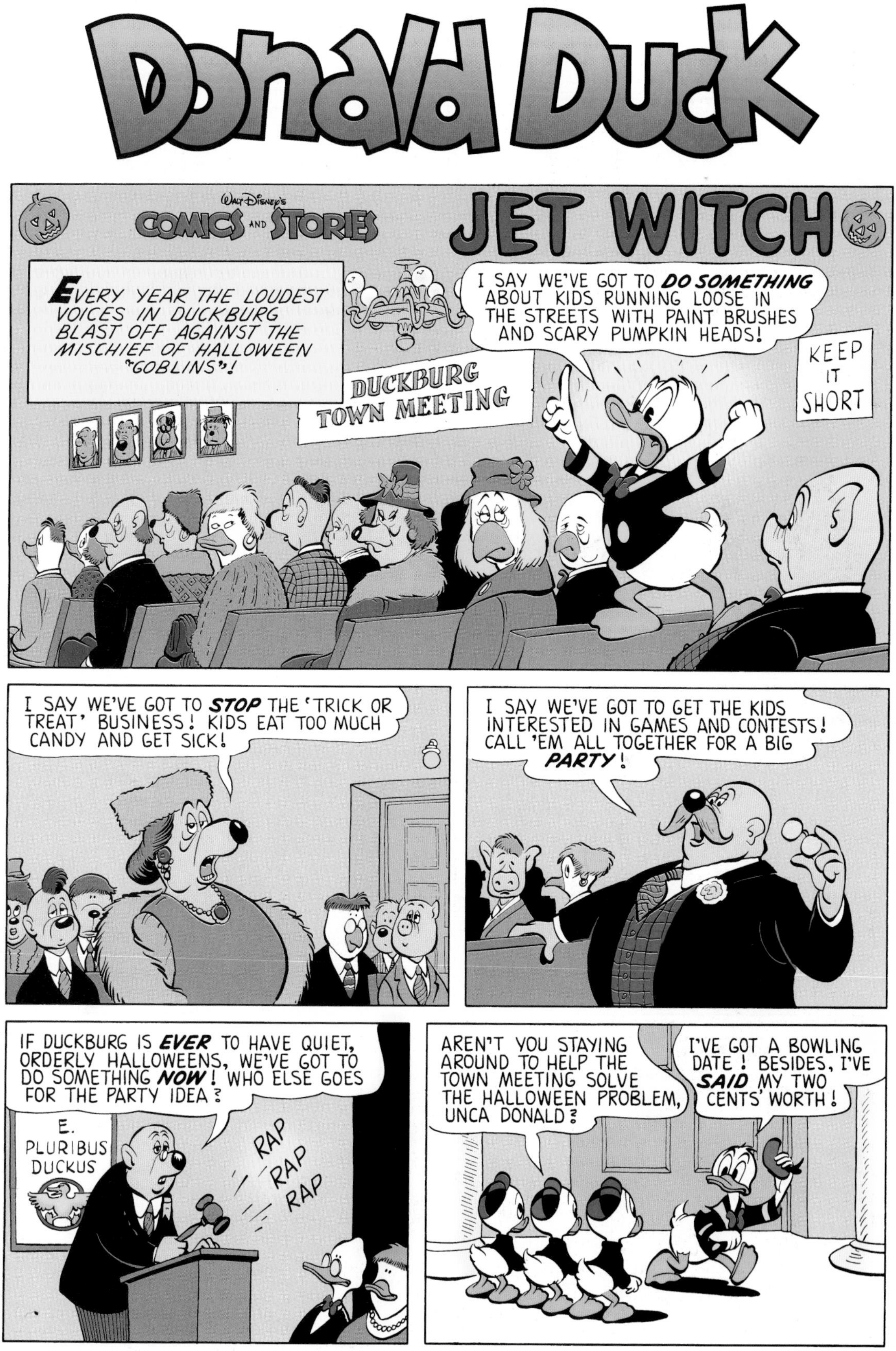
Donald Duck
WALT DISNEY'S COMICS AND STORIES
JET WITCH
EVERY YEAR THE LOUDEST VOICES IN DUCKBURG BLAST OFF AGAINST THE MISCHIEF OF HALLOWEEN "GOBLINS"!
I SAY WE'VE GOT TO DO SOMETHING ABOUT KIDS RUNNING LOOSE IN THE STREETS WITH PAINT BRUSHES AND SCARY PUMPKIN HEADS!
DUCKBURG TOWN MEETING
KEEP IT SHORT
I SAY WE'VE GOT TO STOP THE 'TRICK OR TREAT' BUSINESS! KIDS EAT TOO MUCH CANDY AND GET SICK!
I SAY WE'VE GOT TO GET THE KIDS INTERESTED IN GAMES AND CONTESTS! CALL 'EM ALL TOGETHER FOR A BIG PARTY!
IF DUCKBURG IS EVER TO HAVE QUIET, ORDERLY HALLOWEENS, WE'VE GOT TO DO SOMETHING NOW! WHO ELSE GOES FOR THE PARTY IDEA?
E. PLURIBUS DUCKUS
RAP RAP RAP
AREN'T YOU STAYING AROUND TO HELP THE TOWN MEETING SOLVE THE HALLOWEEN PROBLEM, UNCA DONALD?
I'VE GOT A BOWLING DATE! BESIDES, I'VE SAID MY TWO CENTS' WORTH!

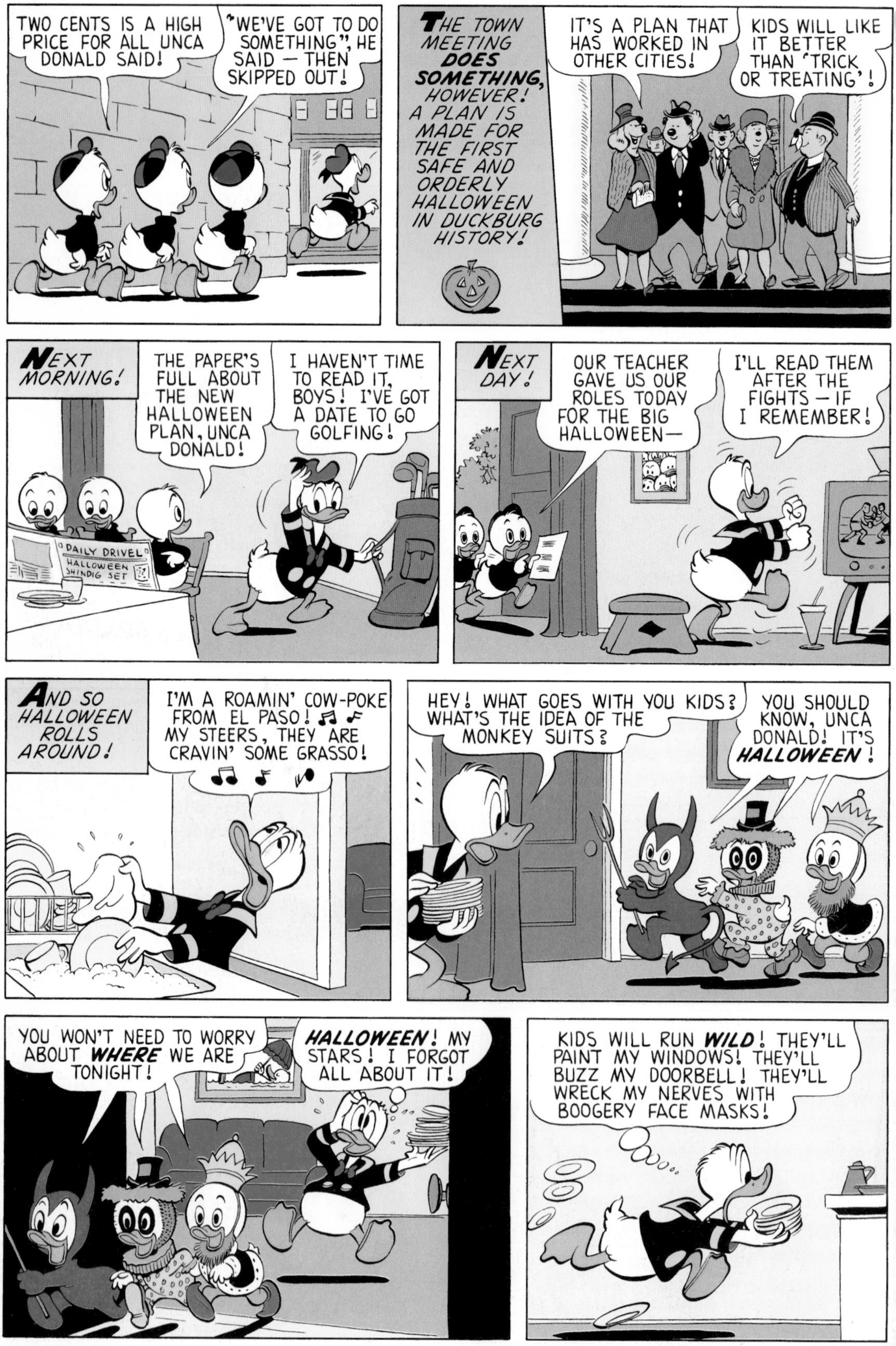
TWO CENTS IS A HIGH PRICE FOR ALL UNCA DONALD SAID!
"WE'VE GOT TO DO SOMETHING", HE SAID — THEN SKIPPED OUT!
THE TOWN MEETING DOES SOMETHING, HOWEVER! A PLAN IS MADE FOR THE FIRST SAFE AND ORDERLY HALLOWEEN IN DUCKBURG HISTORY!
IT'S A PLAN THAT HAS WORKED IN OTHER CITIES!
KIDS WILL LIKE IT BETTER THAN 'TRICK OR TREATING'!
NEXT MORNING!
THE PAPER'S FULL ABOUT THE NEW HALLOWEEN PLAN, UNCA DONALD!
I HAVEN'T TIME TO READ IT, BOYS! I'VE GOT A DATE TO GO GOLFING!
DAILY DRIVEL
HALLOWEEN SHINDIG SET
NEXT DAY!
OUR TEACHER GAVE US OUR ROLES TODAY FOR THE BIG HALLOWEEN—
I'LL READ THEM AFTER THE FIGHTS — IF I REMEMBER!
AND SO HALLOWEEN ROLLS AROUND!
I'M A ROAMIN' COW-POKE FROM EL PASO! MY STEERS, THEY ARE CRAVIN' SOME GRASSO!
HEY! WHAT GOES WITH YOU KIDS? WHAT'S THE IDEA OF THE MONKEY SUITS?
YOU SHOULD KNOW, UNCA DONALD! IT'S HALLOWEEN!
YOU WON'T NEED TO WORRY ABOUT WHERE WE ARE TONIGHT!
HALLOWEEN! MY STARS! I FORGOT ALL ABOUT IT!
KIDS WILL RUN WILD! THEY'LL PAINT MY WINDOWS! THEY'LL BUZZ MY DOORBELL! THEY'LL WRECK MY NERVES WITH BOOGERY FACE MASKS!

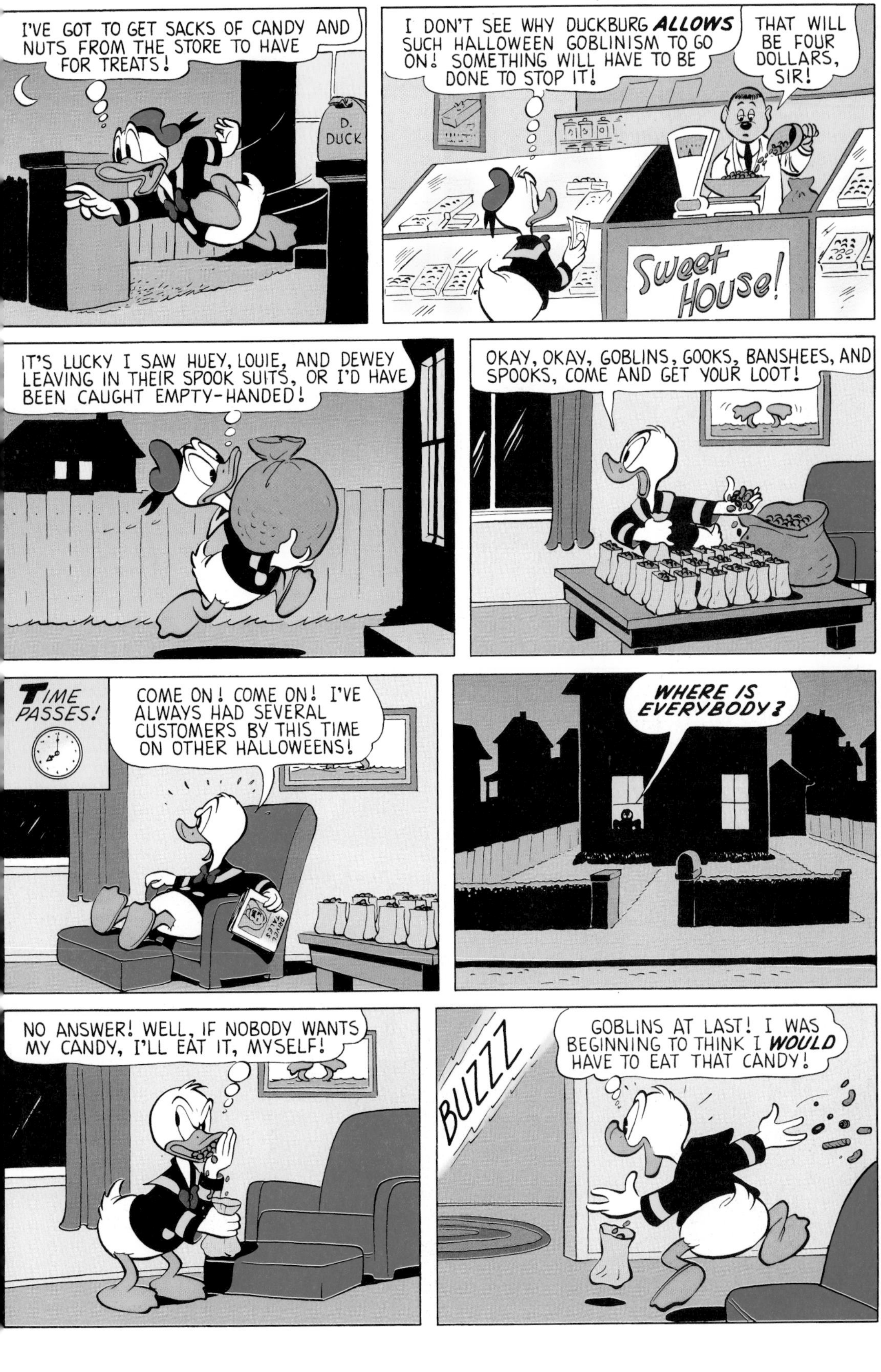
I'VE GOT TO GET SACKS OF CANDY AND NUTS FROM THE STORE TO HAVE FOR TREATS!
D. DUCK
I DON'T SEE WHY DUCKBURG **ALLOWS** SUCH HALLOWEEN GOBLINISM TO GO ON! SOMETHING WILL HAVE TO BE DONE TO STOP IT!
THAT WILL BE FOUR DOLLARS, SIR!
Sweet HOUSE!
IT'S LUCKY I SAW HUEY, LOUIE, AND DEWEY LEAVING IN THEIR SPOOK SUITS, OR I'D HAVE BEEN CAUGHT EMPTY-HANDED!
OKAY, OKAY, GOBLINS, GOOKS, BANSHEES, AND SPOOKS, COME AND GET YOUR LOOT!
TIME PASSES!
COME ON! COME ON! I'VE ALWAYS HAD SEVERAL CUSTOMERS BY THIS TIME ON OTHER HALLOWEENS!
WHERE IS EVERYBODY?
NO ANSWER! WELL, IF NOBODY WANTS MY CANDY, I'LL EAT IT, MYSELF!
BUZZZ
GOBLINS AT LAST! I WAS BEGINNING TO THINK I **WOULD** HAVE TO EAT THAT CANDY!

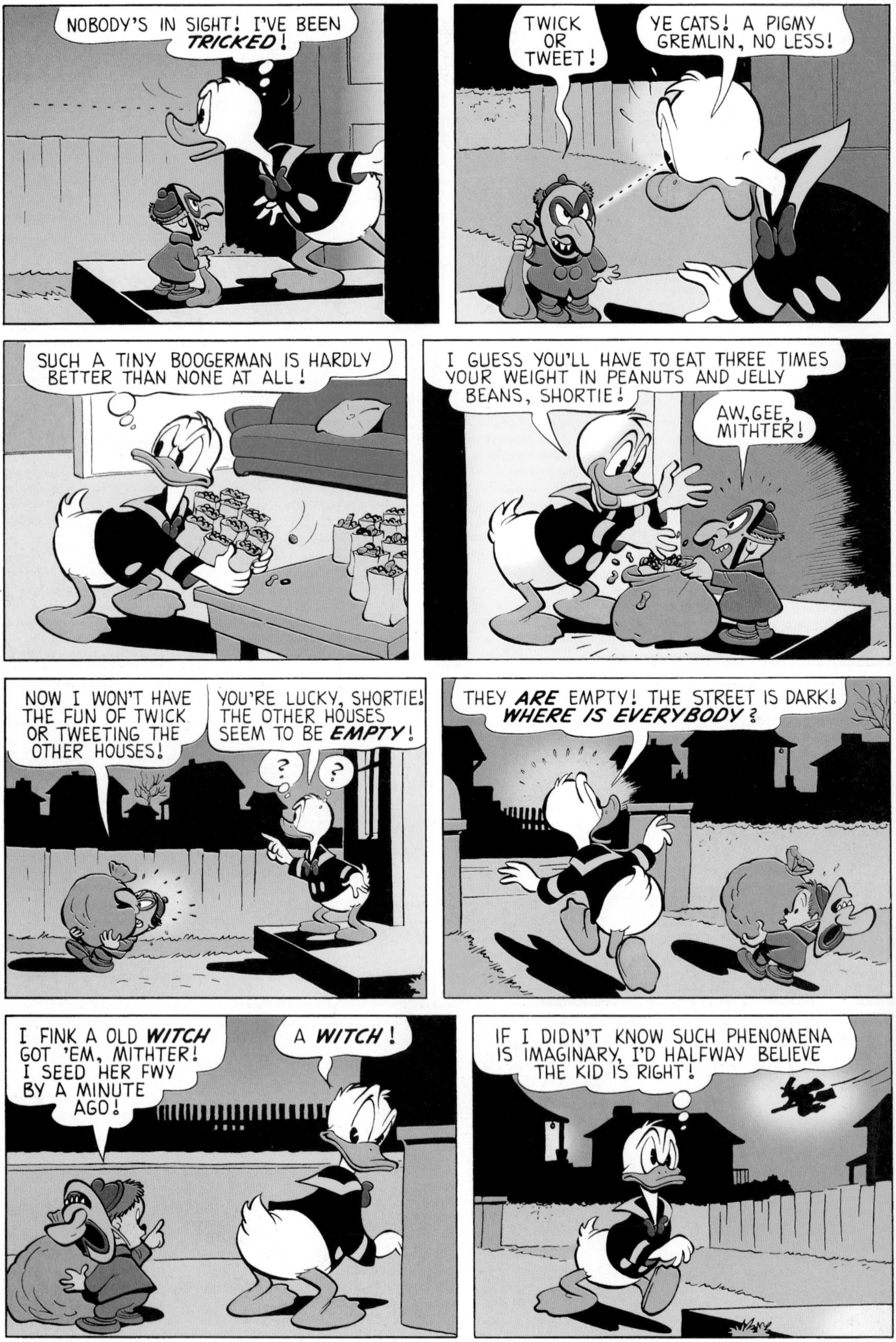
NOBODY'S IN SIGHT! I'VE BEEN *TRICKED*!
TWICK OR TWEET!
YE CATS! A PIGMY GREMLIN, NO LESS!
SUCH A TINY BOOGERMAN IS HARDLY BETTER THAN NONE AT ALL!
I GUESS YOU'LL HAVE TO EAT THREE TIMES YOUR WEIGHT IN PEANUTS AND JELLY BEANS, SHORTIE!
AW, GEE, MITHTER!
NOW I WON'T HAVE THE FUN OF TWICK OR TWEETING THE OTHER HOUSES!
YOU'RE LUCKY, SHORTIE! THE OTHER HOUSES SEEM TO BE *EMPTY*!
THEY *ARE* EMPTY! THE STREET IS DARK! *WHERE IS EVERYBODY*?
I FINK A OLD *WITCH* GOT 'EM, MITHTER! I SEED HER FWY BY A MINUTE AGO!
A *WITCH*!
IF I DIDN'T KNOW SUCH PHENOMENA IS IMAGINARY, I'D HALFWAY BELIEVE THE KID IS RIGHT!

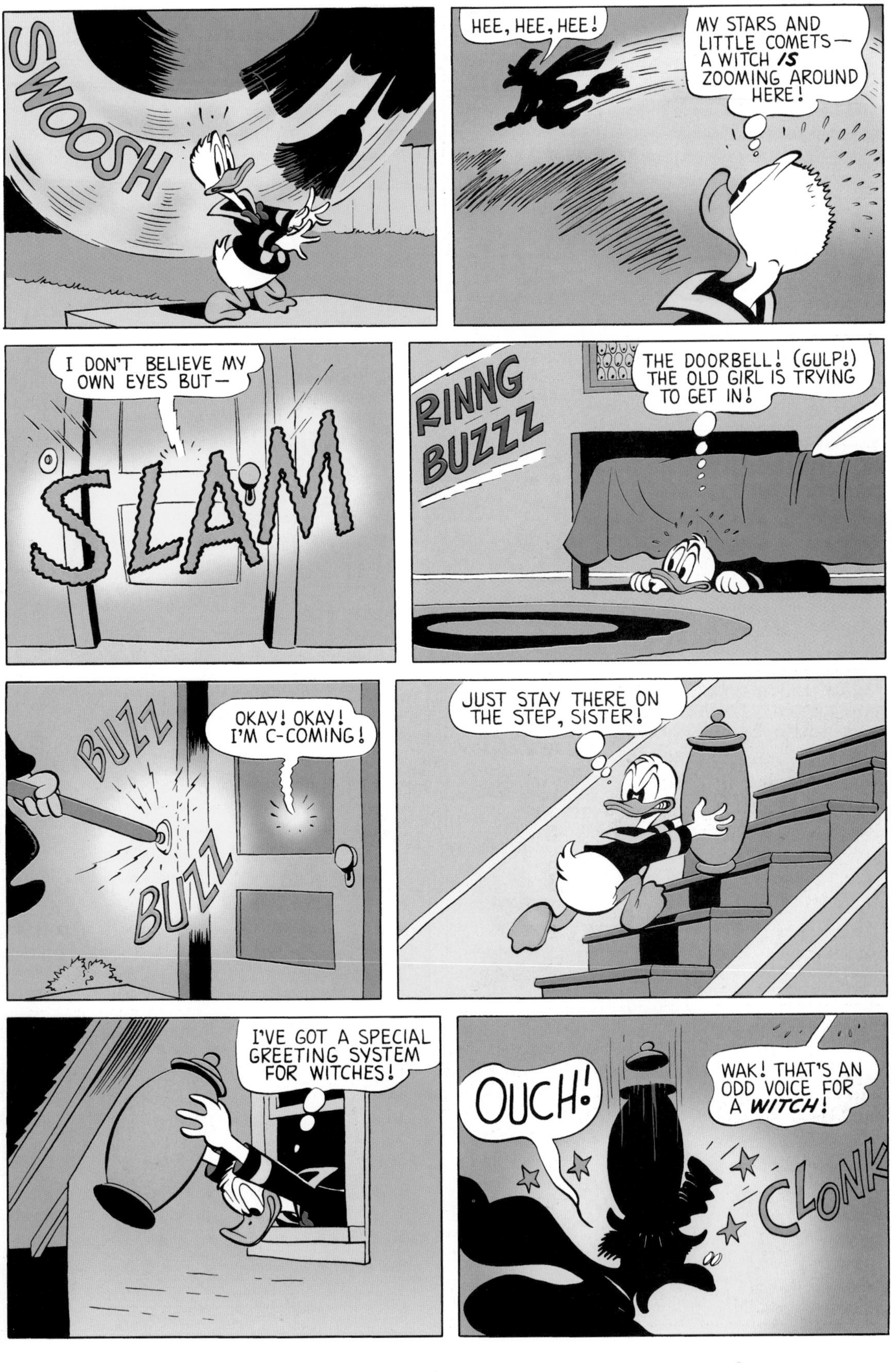
SWOOSH
HEE, HEE, HEE!
MY STARS AND LITTLE COMETS— A WITCH IS ZOOMING AROUND HERE!
I DON'T BELIEVE MY OWN EYES BUT—
SLAM
RINNG BUZZZ
THE DOORBELL! (GULP!) THE OLD GIRL IS TRYING TO GET IN!
BUZZ
BUZZ
OKAY! OKAY! I'M C-COMING!
JUST STAY THERE ON THE STEP, SISTER!
I'VE GOT A SPECIAL GREETING SYSTEM FOR WITCHES!
OUCH!
WAK! THAT'S AN ODD VOICE FOR A WITCH!
CLONK

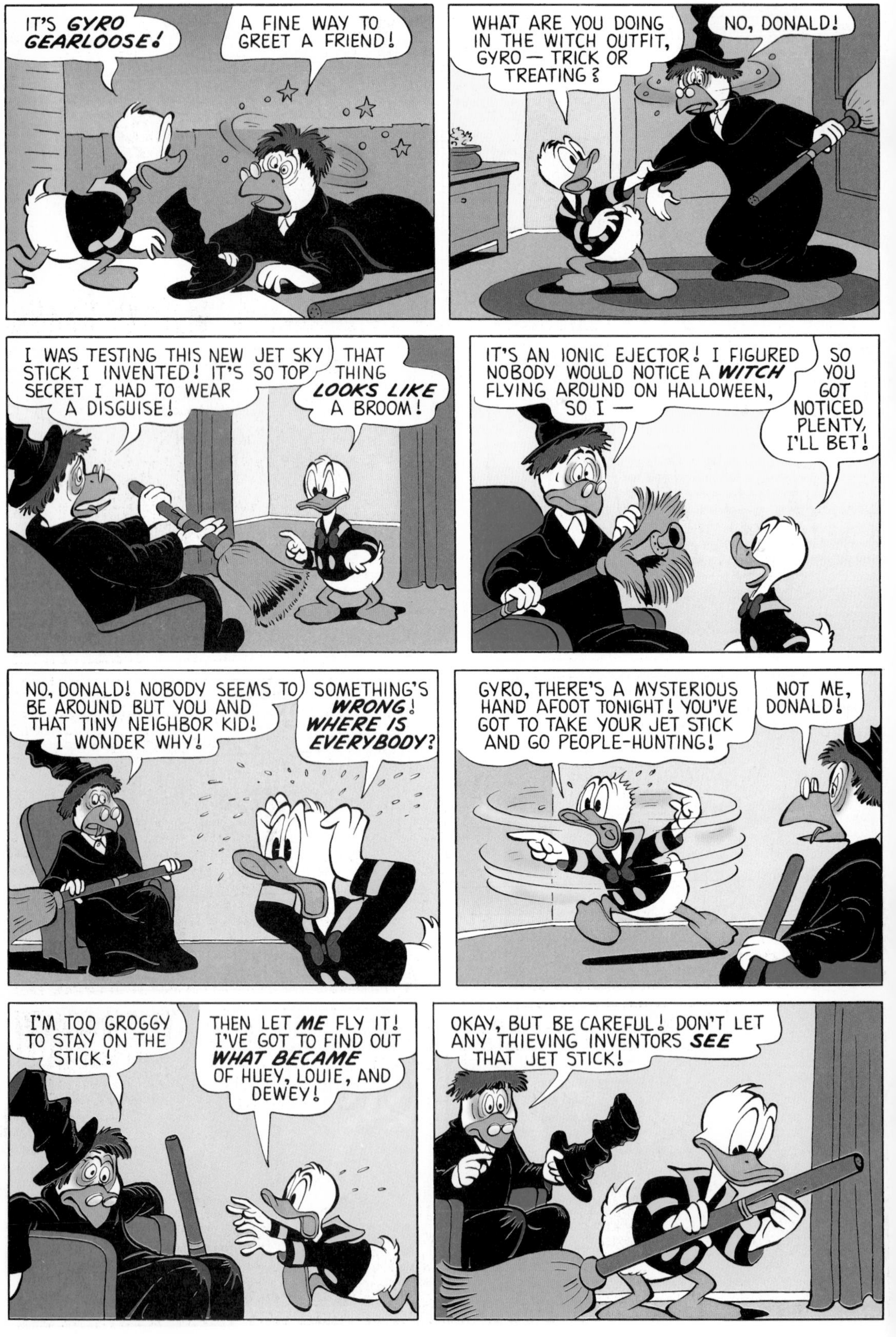

IT'S *GYRO GEARLOOSE!*
A FINE WAY TO GREET A FRIEND!
WHAT ARE YOU DOING IN THE WITCH OUTFIT, GYRO — TRICK OR TREATING?
NO, DONALD!
I WAS TESTING THIS NEW JET SKY STICK I INVENTED! IT'S SO TOP SECRET I HAD TO WEAR A DISGUISE!
THAT THING *LOOKS LIKE* A BROOM!
IT'S AN IONIC EJECTOR! I FIGURED NOBODY WOULD NOTICE A *WITCH* FLYING AROUND ON HALLOWEEN, SO I —
SO YOU GOT NOTICED PLENTY, I'LL BET!
NO, DONALD! NOBODY SEEMS TO BE AROUND BUT YOU AND THAT TINY NEIGHBOR KID! I WONDER WHY!
SOMETHING'S *WRONG*! *WHERE IS EVERYBODY?*
GYRO, THERE'S A MYSTERIOUS HAND AFOOT TONIGHT! YOU'VE GOT TO TAKE YOUR JET STICK AND GO PEOPLE-HUNTING!
NOT ME, DONALD!
I'M TOO GROGGY TO STAY ON THE STICK!
THEN LET *ME* FLY IT! I'VE GOT TO FIND OUT *WHAT BECAME* OF HUEY, LOUIE, AND DEWEY!
OKAY, BUT BE CAREFUL! DON'T LET ANY THIEVING INVENTORS *SEE* THAT JET STICK!

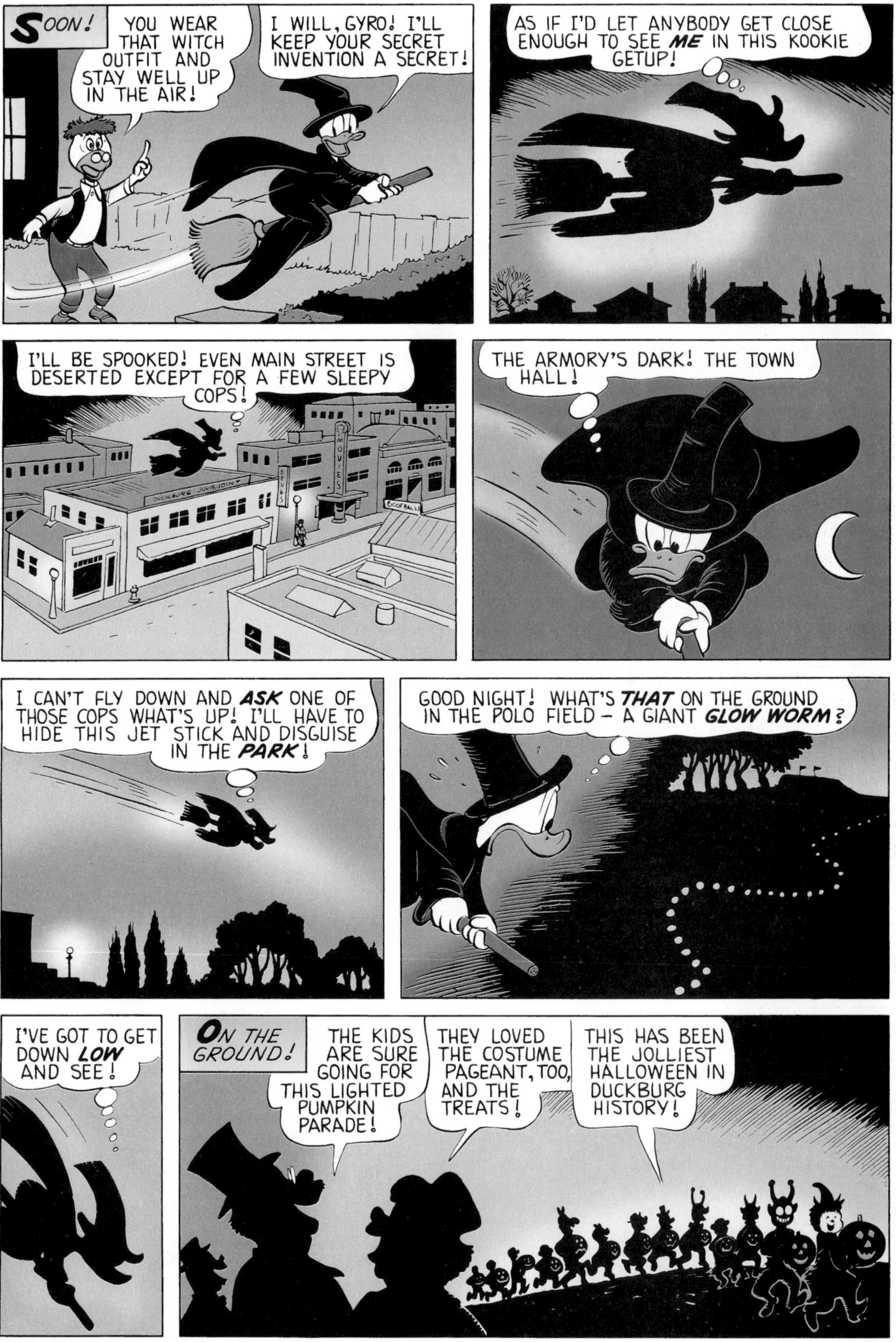
SOON!
YOU WEAR THAT WITCH OUTFIT AND STAY WELL UP IN THE AIR!
I WILL, GYRO! I'LL KEEP YOUR SECRET INVENTION A SECRET!
AS IF I'D LET ANYBODY GET CLOSE ENOUGH TO SEE ME IN THIS KOOKIE GETUP!
I'LL BE SPOOKED! EVEN MAIN STREET IS DESERTED EXCEPT FOR A FEW SLEEPY COPS!
MOVIES
DRUGS
THE ARMORY'S DARK! THE TOWN HALL!
I CAN'T FLY DOWN AND ASK ONE OF THOSE COPS WHAT'S UP! I'LL HAVE TO HIDE THIS JET STICK AND DISGUISE IN THE PARK!
GOOD NIGHT! WHAT'S THAT ON THE GROUND IN THE POLO FIELD – A GIANT GLOW WORM?
I'VE GOT TO GET DOWN LOW AND SEE!
ON THE GROUND!
THE KIDS ARE SURE GOING FOR THIS LIGHTED PUMPKIN PARADE!
THEY LOVED THE COSTUME PAGEANT, TOO, AND THE TREATS!
THIS HAS BEEN THE JOLLIEST HALLOWEEN IN DUCKBURG HISTORY!

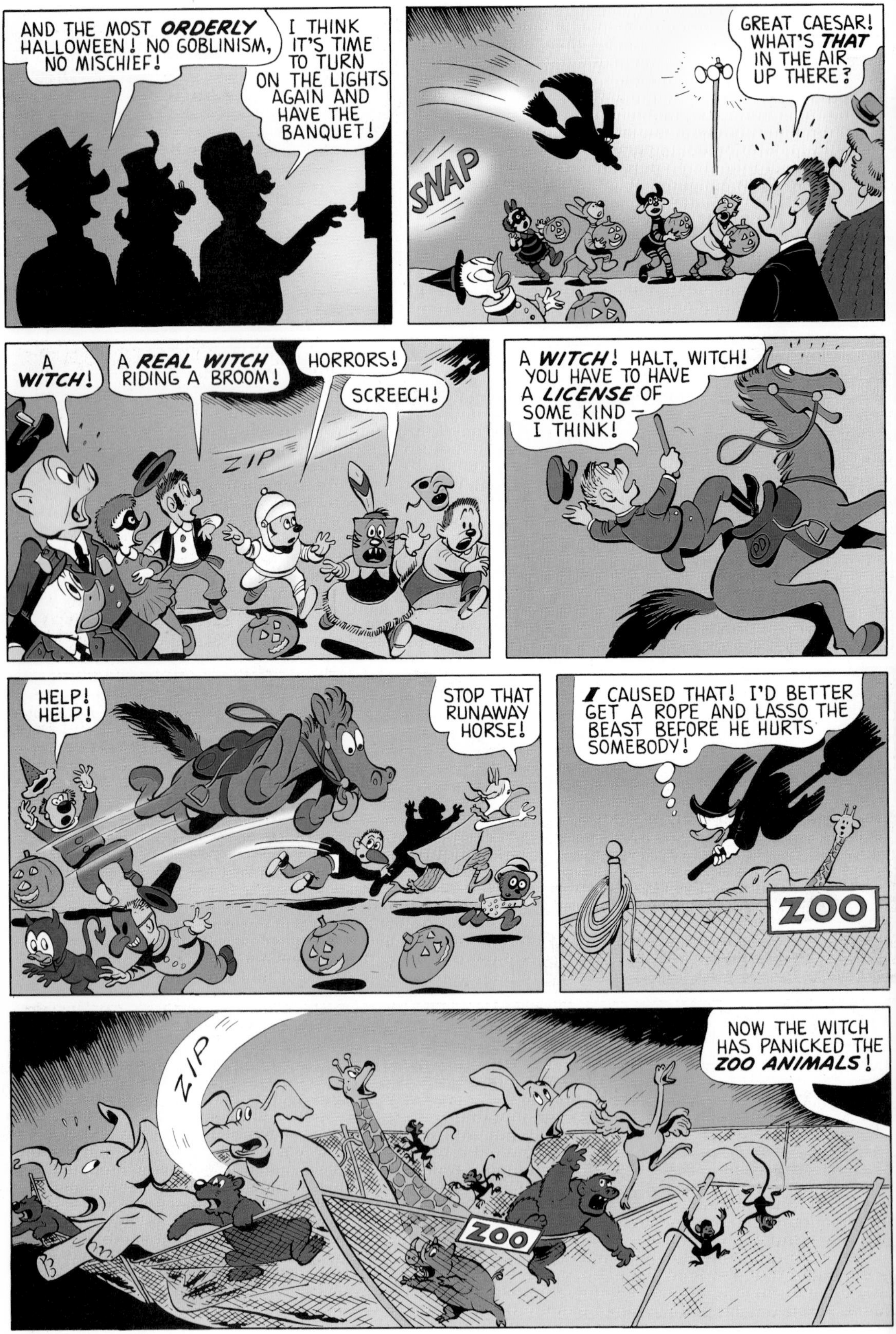

AND THE MOST ORDERLY HALLOWEEN! NO GOBLINISM, NO MISCHIEF!
I THINK IT'S TIME TO TURN ON THE LIGHTS AGAIN AND HAVE THE BANQUET!
SNAP
GREAT CAESAR! WHAT'S THAT IN THE AIR UP THERE?
A WITCH!
A REAL WITCH RIDING A BROOM!
HORRORS!
SCREECH!
ZIP
A WITCH! HALT, WITCH! YOU HAVE TO HAVE A LICENSE OF SOME KIND — I THINK!
PD
HELP! HELP!
STOP THAT RUNAWAY HORSE!
I CAUSED THAT! I'D BETTER GET A ROPE AND LASSO THE BEAST BEFORE HE HURTS SOMEBODY!
ZOO
ZIP
NOW THE WITCH HAS PANICKED THE ZOO ANIMALS!
ZOO

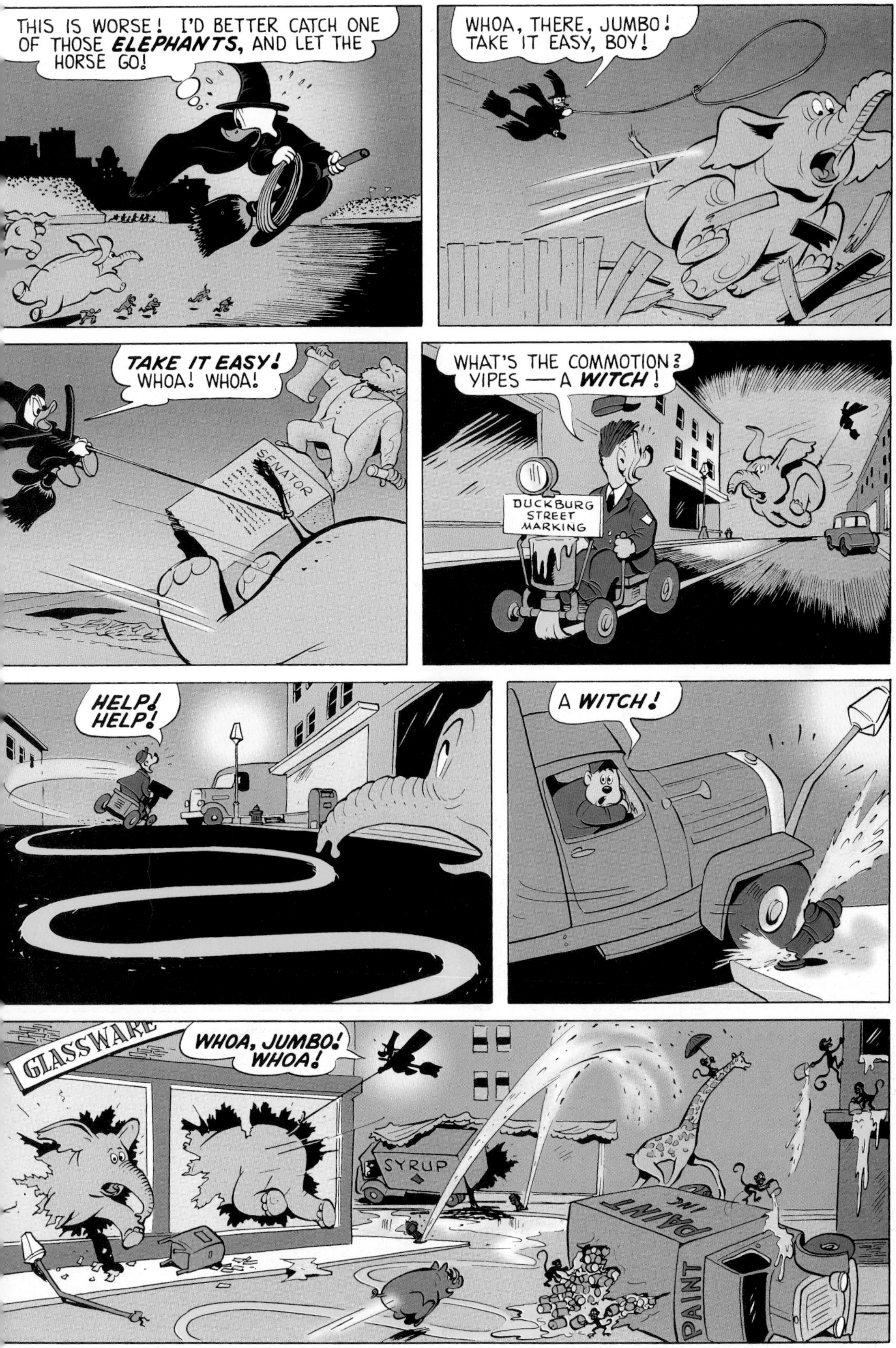
THIS IS WORSE! I'D BETTER CATCH ONE OF THOSE ELEPHANTS, AND LET THE HORSE GO!
WHOA, THERE, JUMBO! TAKE IT EASY, BOY!
TAKE IT EASY! WHOA! WHOA!
SENATOR
WHAT'S THE COMMOTION? YIPES — A WITCH!
DUCKBURG STREET MARKING
HELP! HELP!
A WITCH!
GLASSWARE
WHOA, JUMBO! WHOA!
SYRUP
PAINT INC
PAINT

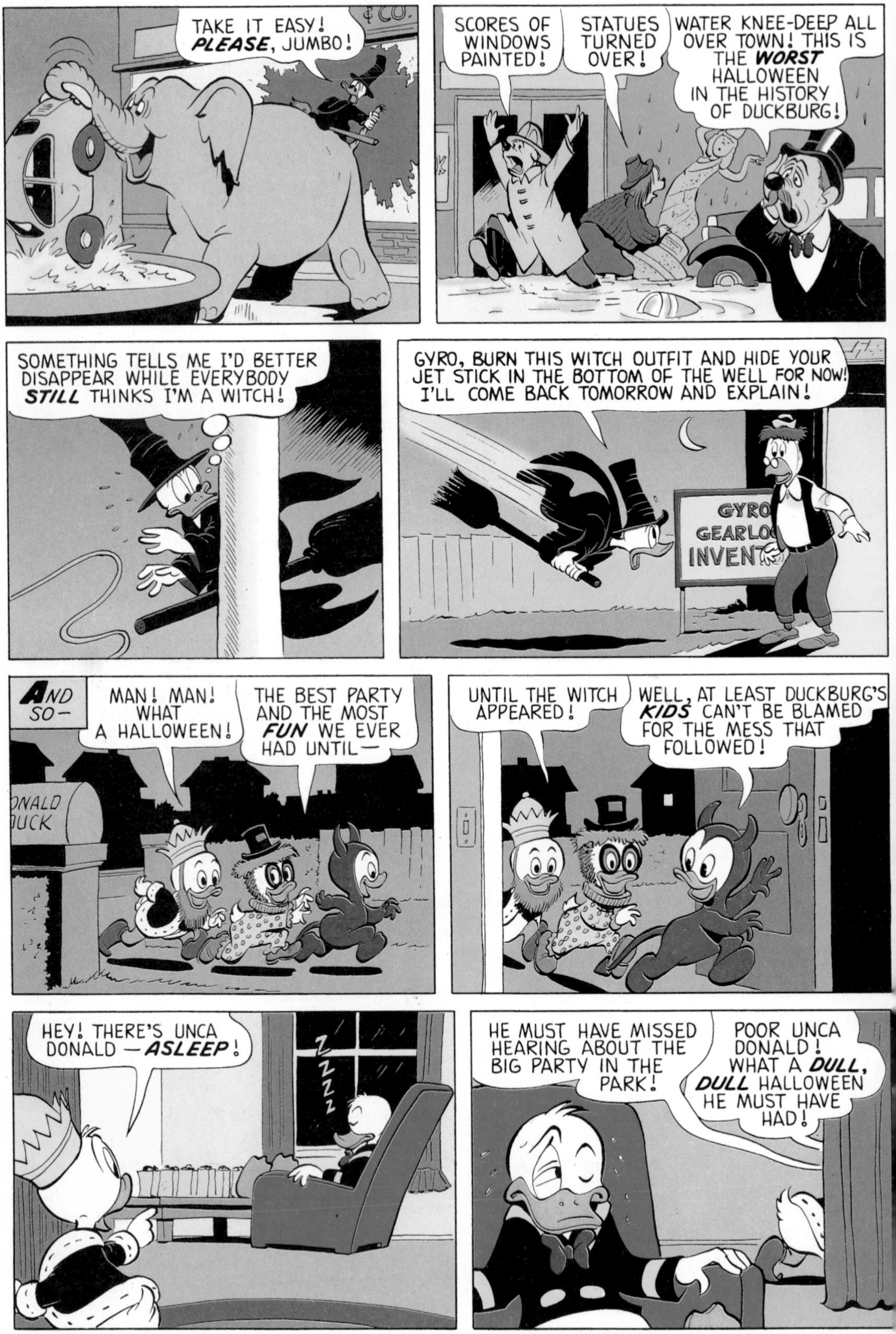
TAKE IT EASY! PLEASE, JUMBO!
SCORES OF WINDOWS PAINTED!
STATUES TURNED OVER!
WATER KNEE-DEEP ALL OVER TOWN! THIS IS THE WORST HALLOWEEN IN THE HISTORY OF DUCKBURG!
SOMETHING TELLS ME I'D BETTER DISAPPEAR WHILE EVERYBODY STILL THINKS I'M A WITCH!
GYRO, BURN THIS WITCH OUTFIT AND HIDE YOUR JET STICK IN THE BOTTOM OF THE WELL FOR NOW! I'LL COME BACK TOMORROW AND EXPLAIN!
GYRO GEARLO INVENT
AND SO—
MAN! MAN! WHAT A HALLOWEEN!
THE BEST PARTY AND THE MOST FUN WE EVER HAD UNTIL—
ONALD UCK
UNTIL THE WITCH APPEARED!
WELL, AT LEAST DUCKBURG'S KIDS CAN'T BE BLAMED FOR THE MESS THAT FOLLOWED!
HEY! THERE'S UNCA DONALD—ASLEEP!
ZZZZ
HE MUST HAVE MISSED HEARING ABOUT THE BIG PARTY IN THE PARK!
POOR UNCA DONALD! WHAT A DULL, DULL HALLOWEEN HE MUST HAVE HAD!